THROWING SHADES

THE DAHLIA WILDES MAGICAL MYSTERIES
BOOK 3

NOVA NELSON

FFS MEDIA

Throwing Shades, The Dahlia Wildes Magical Mysteries #3 / Nova Nelson -- 1st ed.

www.eastwindwitches.com

CHAPTER ONE

Compared to my sweet familiar Atlas, I was incredibly brave. But you wouldn't have known it from the way I acted when I found the dead mouse on the pottery studio floor.

I think the problem might be that I nearly stepped right on the poor little thing as I was groggily making my way past the rows of bisque-fired pots, still half asleep, on my way to open the store for the day. I almost didn't see it until the sole of my boot was only a few inches above it and closing. My brain clicked on, shouted some vague warning at me like, "Fuzzy thing!" and I only just managed to bring my foot down to the side of it.

"Waaaaaaah!" I danced away, flinging my hands in the air. *Fuzzy thing! Not normal!* My brain continued to shout at me like a sleepy cave man.

Atlas, the one out of the two of us less known for courageous acts, was only a few steps behind me and didn't respond well to my little jig. All three hundred pounds of his muscular hellhound body and snow-white fur reared up onto his hind legs, and he practically ran out of the studio like that.

"Atlas, wait!" I felt my brain evolving to understand complex language again. "It's okay. No one is in danger."

Boy, was my heart still racing, though. I tried to catch my breath. Nothing like a jump scare first thing in the morning. Just as well, because I'd failed to stop and grab my morning coffee on the way over.

I caught up to Atlas where he cowered in the back corner of the studio by three large drums of experimental glaze that the studio owners, Jude and Raven, had been tinkering with. His silky white body quivered. "Oh, Atlas," I said, stroking him gently down his neck. "I'm sorry I scared you."

"Is it coming to kill us?" he asked through our telepathic connection.

"No, boy. We're safe. I'm afraid the poor little thing is already dead. It can't hurt anyone."

Atlas peeked his head out from the rest of his white mass, narrowing his eyes at me. *"Did I just hear a witch who can speak to ghosts say we're safe because something is dead?"*

Fair point. "It's just a mouse," I added. "Mice aren't danger—"

"You haven't met a sabertoothed blood mouse, then," he snapped before tucking his head back into his fur. *"The Deadwoods are crawling with them."*

"You're right about one thing: I have no idea what a sabertoothed blood mouse is. I wouldn't mind if it stayed that way, either. But this was just a regular mouse, as far as I could tell. No rodent ghosts floating around to be seen. I'll clean it up and then let you know when the coast is clear, how about that? You can stay right here."

I found a small cloth in one of the supply drawers and returned to the mouse. In a superficial regard, it looked like it was sleeping. But the stillness of death was unmistakable. It wasn't so much something my eyes saw, but something I felt in my skin when I looked at it.

Poor little thing, so tiny and frail. My heart ached in my chest as I knelt down next to it. *What happened to you, little thing?* I wondered. In a pottery studio, it could be a number of things, I supposed.

You'd think I'd be somewhat accustomed to death, being the kind of witch who can speak to spirits and having died once myself, but I wasn't. Even after solving two murders since I first came to town only a handful of months ago, death continued to make me horribly weepy.

I felt the warmth of a tear slip down my cheek as I gazed on the still mouse lying on its side on the cold slab floor, and before I could stop it, the tear broke free, landing on the little critter with the tiniest of splashes. As it soaked into the mouse's fur, I reached down with the cloth to gently scoop up the little being and move it to a better resting place.

But the second my fingertips touched it through the cloth, the little thing twitched, stretched, and then sprang to life. With an adorable squeak, it jumped to its feet and scurried away from me.

"What the—?" I fell backward onto my rear end and watched it run off, hardly believing my own eyes.

I could've sworn it was dead. I felt so certain of it. Clearly I was wrong.

Unless...

No, no, no. What a silly idea. I may not have understood the extent of my powers as a Fifth Wind witch yet, but surely there was no way that I could...

It was too much for my brain, especially this early in the morning.

Maybe, if I were feeling bold enough, I'd consider it later. (I rarely felt bold, so this was an easy way to put off thinking about it.) Or maybe I ought to ask Nora about it. She'd been a Fifth Wind witch much longer than me and had experience with all kinds of strange powers. She would know. And if she didn't know, her mentor, Ruby, would.

And they'll both tell you that the mouse was simply asleep, not dead. I forced that reassuring thought to be the end of it. No reason to make a big deal out of the encounter anyway.

As my adrenaline wore off, I assured Atlas the coast was clear, neglecting to mention that the mouse could be anywhere, alive and well.

He stuck closely to my side as we continued on through the studio, passing the rows of pottery wheels that would be busy with students during early classes in a few hours, and making our way into the shop portion of Time to Kiln.

I flipped the sign to open, but didn't expect anyone to show up right away. That was ideal. I was paid by the hour, and the delay in customers meant I had some quiet time each morning to settle into the day.

The shop was a wonderful place to spend a quiet morning. It had massive display windows all around, and on a sunny day, the dawn light reflected beautifully off the glazes of the stoneware items on offering, painting the floor and walls in a rainbow watercolor.

Today was not one of those sunny days, though.

The chilly February wind whistled at the front windows of the shop. I walked to the window displays and peered outside between the vases and teapots lining the shelves. Sure enough, the sky was still a thick blanket of gray, and I wondered if my plans for that afternoon would be cancelled as a result. Surely something called the Blue Sky Festival needed blue skies. A cancellation would be such a shame. I'd been looking forward to the outing with Dante since he told me all about it weeks ago. It was a big deal in Eastwind. Everyone would be there, and since I'd been in town just over three months and had worked in this shop where I met new people every day, I was starting to feel like I belonged. This would be my first town gathering where I would recognize a good number of folks and they would recognize me back, maybe even know my name. I'd secretly been looking forward to such a thing for the last few weeks. But with these gray skies threatening even more snow than we'd had over the last few weeks...

I sighed and returned to opening the shop.

My place behind a small counter in the corner opposite the front door was starting to feel familiar after my months of working here. It was a little cozy nook with a solid view of the whole place. I was able to see who came in and left the shop as well as who walked into the shop from the studio in the back half of the building. It allowed me to enjoy two of my favorite pastimes: observing people and staying out of the way. I had a fantastic view through the large windows that looked out onto the cobblestone streets of Eastwind. Optimal people watching. I'd been a semi-professional people watcher since long before I died and came to Eastwind.

The only problem with people watching is that sometimes it makes you forget that you, too, are a person. You start to feel like an outsider observing humanity rather than an integral part of it. You forgot that as you were watching others, one of them might also be watching you.

Staring aimlessly out onto the street, my mind wandered back to the mouse. How had it gotten there, poor thing? Atlas hadn't killed it. (*Because it wasn't dead, Dahlia.*) Had it been sleeping? Was it sick? Had it gotten into one of the glazes? From what I understood, many of those were toxic, and if the chemicals didn't get you, the magic in them might. Jude, the werewolf who owned the place with his best friend Raven, swore that a mouse had been transformed into a handsome man years ago after getting into two different experimental glazes. Raven, a boisterous South Wind witch who rarely let her feelings go unexpressed, always rolled her eyes when he told that story, though, so I wasn't entirely sure it was true.

The door to the shop opened, the sound of the bell above it nudging me out of my own head, and despite the cold draft that entered with the newcomers, I felt warmth wash through me as I saw who it was.

CHAPTER TWO

Landon Hawker's cheeks were rosy from the cold as he gripped his son Monty's hand and gently reminded him that there was lots of delicate stuff in the shop so he needed to keep holding daddy's hand. Landon, a nerdy but kind-hearted North Wind witch, was a few years older than me, but with his rosy cheeks and boyish curiosity that kept his eyes wide behind his glasses, he looked like he could be in his early twenties. I wasn't sure how one could continue to appear so youthful while raising a small child. The fact that Monty was a werewolf added its own unique challenges in rearing him for the last five years. Following closely behind the pair was Grace Merryweather, one of my closest friends in Eastwind and Monty's mother. She smiled at me as she stepped inside behind her husband. The door would've closed on its own, but she gave it a tug to speed up the process. "We're heading down to Medium Rare for breakfast," she said. "Thought we'd stop in and see if you wanted us to bring you anything back."

"Oh no, I'm fine," I replied.

Grace sighed, stomped her boots on the entry mat to relieve them of a few chunks of snow, then confidently approached me at the desk. "Would you even tell me if you weren't fine? Really, it's not a problem. We can pick up something for you while we're there. If we tell Nora it's for you, she likely won't even charge us."

A coffee and some bacon did sound nice, I couldn't deny that.

Before I could answer, Atlas lumbered to his feet from beneath my desk and peeked out at the new arrivals. Monty squealed with delight. "Atwahs!"

Over the last couple of months, the two of them had formed a unique friendship. Though Monty was five years old, he wasn't particularly verbal, something Grace had mentioned to me one day as we threw on potters' wheels across from each other. It wasn't a major concern, she explained. Children developed in their own time and their own way. I didn't mention to her that I could feel her maternal angst about it breaking through her calm façade. So instead, I'd told her that he was very lucky to have such an accepting mother who learned all she could about him.

As a result of his lack of verbal skills, Monty didn't interact with many of the other children his age in Eastwind, of which there were few to start with in such a small town. He much preferred animals, and atop his list of animals was Atlas.

The hellhound was still terrified of most children, insisting that they would bop him on the head without a moment's hesitation. But for some inexplicable reason, that fear didn't extend to Monty... who immediately bopped Atlas on the head whenever he saw him. Not hard, but with the jerky head pats of a wild child, which Monty most definitely was.

This morning was no exception, and as soon as Atlas was within reach of Monty, whose hand continued to be gripped tightly in Landon's like a makeshift leash, the child bopped the hellhound repeatedly between the ears. Atlas simply wagged his tail.

Their exchanges made me smile every time, and before long, Monty was riding on Atlas's back in circles around the shop, giggling and holding on tight to the fur between the hellhound's shoulders. Landon hovered close, ready to catch the boy if he fell, though that had never happened in the many times I'd seen them play this game.

"Maybe some bacon for Atlas," I said, continuing our interrupted conversation.

When I turned my attention from the fun to Grace, she was frowning at me.

"What? What's that face about?"

She squinted at me like I was a sphinx's riddle. "How come you can ask for breakfast for Atlas but not for yourself?"

"Because I'm fine." I shrugged. I had every intention of stealing a few strips of bacon for myself before giving any to Atlas, though.

"You're not. Excuse my frankness, but when we walked in here, you looked half asleep. You *clearly* could use some of that spitfire Medium Rare coffee, and I've offered it. Why is it so hard for you to accept a favor?"

I opened my mouth to answer, but nothing intelligent came to mind, so I settled with. "I don't know. Isn't it hard for everyone?"

"Not me," she said flatly. "If one of my friends offers me

something and I would like to have what they're offering, I say yes."

"But what if you don't know that they really mean it? What if they're only offering to be nice?"

She arched a brow at me. "You think I feel *obligated* to offer you food? You know this shop isn't technically along our route to the Outskirts. We took a side street to get here. We could've just walked straight to breakfast and you'd have never known the difference. But we didn't, because I knew you had to open early, and you're bad about getting yourself breakfast and coffee when you need it. So I thought I would drop by and offer to get you something. You know, like friends do."

I held up my hands in surrender. "Okay, okay. Sure. Fine. Coffee and bacon sounds fabulous."

She nodded once. "That's what I thought." A small grin turned the corners of her lips. "Next time, please make it easier to be your friend."

I laughed. Grace's directness was one of the things I liked most about her. That and the fact that she was one of the least emotional people I knew. As someone whose powers included feeling the strong emotions of those around me, I found it incredibly soothing to be in the presence of someone with true equanimity. "I'll try," I said.

"There will be plenty of food at the Blue Sky Festival this afternoon, but we'll make sure you have enough to tide you over." She paused. "You're going to that, right?"

"Is it still happening? I don't see any signs of the clouds letting up."

Landon was the one to answer, though he kept his eyes glued firmly on Monty and Atlas as he did. "Don't worry about that," he said. "We have more than enough North

Wind witches in this town to clear out the clouds as needed."

Both Landon and Grace were North Winds, sometimes called Aeromancers because of their special powers related to the air and sky, so I trusted them as experts on that matter.

"It'll be nice to see a blue sky again after so long," I said.

"That's the point of the festival," Grace replied. "Sometimes winter really overstays its welcome. A little blue sky can go a long way toward keeping spirits up until spring." She paused. "Coffee and bacon for you and bacon for Atlas. It that all?"

"That's more than plenty," I said. "And thank you."

She shot me a thumbs up and turned to leave.

Landon scooped Monty off Atlas's back, waved goodbye, and I watched the three of them step out onto the street and head toward the Outskirts to enjoy a family breakfast at Medium Rare. I could already see Monty throwing bits of cut-up steak and eggs—his favorite breakfast—on the checkerboard tile of the diner while Landon calmly explained that food goes in the mouth, not on the floor.

Grim, Nora's familiar who spent most of his time being hand-fed by enamored patrons at the diner, loved Monty almost as much as Atlas did, but for different reasons. In my imagined family meal, I could already see the big, black hellhound cleaning off the floor by Monty's feet. Few things were more symbiotic than a small child during a meal and a dog who liked scraps.

Atlas padded over to his spot behind the desk and flopped down at my feet with a sigh. *"Good kid, that one."*

"Are you partial to him because he's a werewolf?" I asked.

"Hadn't thought of it, but maybe."

Atlas had spent a lot of time around werewolves in their wolf forms during his years in the Deadwoods, but those years had also been so traumatic for him that I usually avoided bringing them up. When living in a terrain that favors darkness and shadows, being stark white is quite the unfair hand to be dealt, and Atlas had a pawful of those cards.

A few minutes later, the door opened again, and in popped another familiar face. It wasn't one I was used to seeing outside of grim contexts, but I was happy to see him all the same.

"Ted," I said, "what brings you in?"

The town's grim reaper, wearing his usual black cloak that obscured his face, waved a gloved hand. "Buggy," he replied. "It's her birthday, and I wanted to get her something nice. I thought an offering bowl would be appropriate. Heh."

"Her... birthday?" Buggy, whose full name was Mudbug, had once been the familiar of a particularly evil witch. Nowadays, she was a ghost and Ted's unofficial pet. I doubted she thought of herself as a "pet," but she was certainly bonded to him, more like a familiar than anything else.

Ted shrugged. "We don't know for sure when her birthday is, so we just picked one. My favorite number is two and hers is three, so we went with February third."

"That's very sweet," I said. "The offering bowls are over here."

A lot of Eastwinders didn't enjoy being in proximity to

Ted. He sent a chill of death through them, reminding them of their own mortality. That wasn't what I got off him, though. I found his presence peaceful, so I didn't mind that he followed so closely behind as I led him to the shelf with the offering bowls.

"Oooh," he said, "these are pretty! She'll love one of these. Any magical properties I should know about?"

I pointed to one with a blue glaze so dark it reminded me of the deep ocean. "That one offers the deceased tranquility." Pointing to green one, I said, "That one offers fulfillment and spiritual regeneration."

"What about that one?" he said, gesturing to a pearly pink one.

"That one makes the deceased feel a wave of love whenever an offering is added."

He made a rasping sound like a blade being dragged along a rusty washboard, which I took to be a delighted gasp. "Oh, Buggy *definitely* deserves to feel more loved."

"To be honest, I'm not sure that it works. Raven is a talented witch, but who's to say that any magic at all could produce those feelings for a spirit that's crossed over?"

Ted waved it off. "It doesn't matter if it works or not. Buggy's still earthbound anyway. Even if the magic doesn't hold, I think she'll like the color and when I pour some milk in there for her, I imagine she'll feel loved, even if she can't drink it."

I could feel Ted's love for his ghost cat spilling from him just in our conversation, so I knew he had a point. Magic or not, the gift itself would make Buggy feel loved.

As I finished up Ted's transaction, which included wrapping the gift (I added a more elaborate bow to the box than I was supposed to), Grace popped back in again. She seemed in a hurry. "Monty's having a meltdown," she explained, nodding to the street where Landon hunched over the child who had collapsed into a pile on the cobblestones.

"Oh no," I said. "What's wrong?"

She shrugged. "He started shifting form in his booster seat at the diner. When Landon asked him to please wait until he was done eating before turning his hands into paws, *this* started." She placed the to-go box and coffee cup on the counter, and my eyes nearly rolled back in my head when I caught my first whiff of the food.

"Shifting already?" Ted said. "Precocious!"

Grace sighed heavily. "That's our kid. Five years old, already reading in multiple languages, and shifting at restaurants."

I patted the to-go box. "Thank you. I'll see you this afternoon?"

"If we can get Monty to go down for a nap, yes. These big developmental phases wreak havoc on his sleep schedule."

"Poor little guy," crooned Ted.

"You say that *now*," Grace replied, "but in ten years, he'll be a teen wolf terrorizing your neck of the Deadwoods. I hope you're ready."

Ted shot her a thumbs up. "I always enjoy visitors at my cabin."

"With the way things are going, you won't want to let him inside. He'll find some way to burn down the place."

"Oh, that's not a problem." Ted dismissed the concern with a flick of his wrist. "The place is fireproof. Kind of a requirement when you raise phoenixes. Heh."

Once Grace was back on the street, helping Landon

wrangle their kid, Ted turned to me. "You're going to the Blue Sky Festival?"

"Yep. We're closing early." I checked the clock on the wall. "Dante should be by in a couple hours, and we'll walk over together. You're going?"

"Of course! I wouldn't miss a Blue Sky Festival for anything. Everyone's in such great spirits. I'll celebrate Buggy's birthday with her and then we'll head over."

"Great, see you then!"

Ted tucked the gift box under his arm, disappearing it into the loose black fabric of his robes, and headed out, leaving me temporarily alone in the shop to enjoy my breakfast.

Atlas's head flopped onto the desktop.

Oh right. Not alone.

When I opened the to-go box, there wasn't just bacon inside, but a few biscuits as well. She didn't have to do that.

But I was glad she did.

A perk of working at a pottery studio was that there were always spare plates around: ones students made that didn't turn out the way they'd planned and were therefore donated as studio property. I just had to be sure the one I selected from the cupboard wasn't enchanted before I ate off it. Mostly, everyone knew to keep the enchanted community dishes separate from the ordinary ones, but I was pretty sure I'd eaten from a misplaced spelled one the week before. It caused my sandwich to taste like cake. Not the worst outcome, considering, but I wanted this bacon to taste like bacon, so I was as careful as I could be when I grabbed two plates from the kitchenette in the back, piled most of the bacon on one, set that down for Atlas, and then piled what was left onto a plate with the biscuits for me.

The coffee had just the right amount of cream and sugar in it, which brought a smile to my face. There was no doubt that Grace had told Nora who the to-go order was for, and Nora had made my coffee just how I liked it.

I spread the included butter and jelly on the biscuits and took my first bite. Still warm. I moaned as the flaky layers melted in my mouth.

Chewing slowly, eyes closed, I soaked up the indulgence of what some might call a simple breakfast. For me, though, simple was decadent. How many mornings in New Orleans had I skipped breakfast, either because I was in a rush to get out the door or because I simply didn't have enough money to eat three meals a day and breakfast felt the easiest to skip? I hadn't fully broken the habit since coming to Eastwind, but if anything would convince me to prioritize the most important meal of the day, it was these biscuits and bacon.

As I slowly came out of my reverie, it occurred to me how strange it felt to have people in my life who simply wanted to take good care of me. While I understood *my* impulse to care for those in my life, I couldn't fathom why anyone would bother doing the same in return. I certainly wouldn't blame them if they didn't. Truly, I was no one special. And yet, friends like Grace and Nora treated me as if I were someone *very* special. At least to them.

The next two hours passed in a blur, as the store activity picked up substantially in the later part of the morning. I was deeply grateful to have had a solid meal ahead of it.

Raven had warned me the day before that it might be this busy; tankards were a big part of the Blue Sky Festival as everyone toasted to brighter days, and Raven's ceramic tankards were undeniably gorgeous. She'd prepared extra ahead of the expected rush, and it was no surprise that the ones with the powder-blue glaze and a bright orange sun symbol were flying off the shelves. I could hardly keep up with restocking them while also ringing up the purchases.

Since I'd been in town less than a year, I didn't know what winters in Eastwind were usually like, but I'd heard from plenty of people that this one had felt especially long and dreary. I'd felt as much coming off people, too, any time I made my way through crowds in the Emporium or ate at packed restaurants.

The emotions filling the shop now were quite different, though—excitement and hope. It felt contagious and not just because my powers meant I absorbed the emotions of those around me through my magic. *Everyone* seemed to be feeding off each other's emotions today. I couldn't stop grinning as I helped each customer.

The morning flew by so quickly that I didn't realize it was time to close for the day until I saw Dante walk in. He looked around at the shoppers, said hello to a few, and then made his way over to me. "I thought you were closing early today."

"I am," I said. "Just lost track of time. I should've closed ten minutes ago."

He nodded and took it upon himself to flip the sign in the window from *open* to *closed* while I rang up the next costumer.

Atlas joined Dante by the front door, clearly expecting to get some head scratches out of it. He was right about that. Dante had more than earned Atlas's trust, which was not easily given, and it gave me butterflies to see the man—werebear, if we're being technical—that I had such strong feelings for being so kind and gentle with my familiar. In the relatively short time I'd spent in Eastwind, I'd fallen so hard for Atlas that he was starting to feel like an extension of me. I hoped that was normal for witches and that I wasn't being overbearing, but either way, it was the truth. He felt less like my familiar than he did my other half. And because of that, someone earning the trust of Atlas was about the biggest green flag I knew of. As far as I could tell, Dante was a giant walking green flag. I mean, sure, he got into a few scuffles now and again, but they were usually for the right reasons.

I finished counting up the coins from the day and stored them in a safe in the back of the studio before joining Dante in the shop. "All done. Sorry about running behind." I cringed apologetically.

"Don't sweat it," he said, scratching Atlas behind the ears. "We still have plenty of time before the feast. That's the main event of the festival anyway."

I felt a ball of tension in my chest relax, knowing he wasn't upset about the delay.

He held the door open for me as I stepped outside, and I locked the shop and slipped the small key ring into my pocket. It only held three keys—one each for the front and back doors of Time to Kiln and one for Nora and Tanner's house where I was staying—so it fit easily into the pocket of my wool coat.

Dante offered the crook of his arm, and I gladly accepted it, gripping his bicep with both hands to keep them warm.

He looked down at them. "You forgot gloves?"

I blushed. "Yeah. Overslept this morning and rushed out of the house without them."

He placed a large hand over one of mine. "I don't mind helping you keep them warm."

My stomach flip-flopped when our eyes met, and I hoped I wasn't grinning like a fool. I probably was.

"It'll be warmer soon," he added, nodding toward the sky. "Look, there's already a break in the clouds."

Sure enough, the gray sky was opening up.

"The North Winds are talented," I said. "It felt like the clouds would never budge."

He pressed his elbow close to his body, squeezing my hands against his side. "They always do eventually."

It hadn't snowed the night before, and what drifts were left from earlier in the week were quickly growing into muddy messes along the edges of the cobblestone streets. Atlas went and peed on one, adding some dashes of yellow to the mix. My familiar had expressed on more than one occasion that he wasn't thrilled with the disappearance of snow, since it provided such good camouflage for his white coat. Blending in made him feel safer than anything, and he'd developed some solid stealth skills during the snowy months. He'd even managed to sneak up on Grim a few times, causing the other hellhound to yip with surprise and scuttle away a few steps with his tail between his legs. That inevitably led to the two hounds roughhousing for a while, which was fine as long as they had plenty of space for it. It also brought Nora and me to tears with laughter.

While I was glad for the promise of a warmer day once the sun was able to shine through, I also felt slightly bad for Atlas, who might soon see these last bits of snow disappear.

"You know," Dante said, alerting me to just how much my mind was wandering on our walk, "I really enjoy the time we spend together."

I felt my cheeks heat up. "Yeah, me too."

"And we spend a lot of time together."

Not sure where he was going, I nodded but stayed silent so he would continue.

"I think it's pretty clear how I feel about you," he said, "and I don't mean to be presumptuous, but I think you feel the same about me."

Where on earth was he going with this?

He went on. "Most women I know would want some kind of, I dunno, *commitment* at this point. They might be looking to put labels on it, you know?"

"Mm-hm," I said, trying to sound as neutral as possible. But seriously, where was he going with this?

He hugged my hands closer to his body. "I guess I'm mentioning it to see if you also want that."

"What do you mean?" I steadied my gaze on the street in front of us, unsure why this was making me so nervous.

I knew what he meant, by the way. I just felt myself freezing, felt my brain turning foggy. It was so silly to feel like that, though, wasn't it? Dante liked me. We'd shared our first kiss just over a month ago, and that hadn't been our last.

"Are you the kind of person who wants labels on a relationship?" he said.

For how rapidly my heart was beating, you'd think I was being chased through the Deadwoods by a rabid werebunny. I did my best to at least appear calm, though.

"Labels like what?" I asked. Yes, I was delaying having to answer, but also, my brain was having trouble forming words. My mouth felt suddenly dry, and I didn't think it was from the cool air.

"Like boyfriend and girlfriend," he answered simply.

Was his heart not pounding a thousand beats per minute in his chest right now? How could he sound so calm and confident about this conversation?

You're a grown woman, Dahlia. Relax. Adults have this kind of conversation. It's normal. That's why he sounds relaxed.

I tried to tune into his emotions to get a read on how he was feeling, but mine were too intense for me to feel beyond them.

What did he want me to say? Did he *want* to be my boyfriend? Did he *want* me to be his girlfriend? Or did he phrase it as "most women would want," because he *didn't* like that most women wanted a label?

With my brain a frazzled and muddy mess, I went with the only answer I could think of: "Oh. Um. What we have right now is fine. If you're fine with it, so am I. We don't have to define anything if you don't want."

I could feel him staring down at me, but I kept my gaze focused ahead so as not to let on about how my brain had turned to mush as my body was telling me to make a break for it to the nearest forest without looking back.

"Okay, then." He exhaled deeply. "If you want to keep it as two people enjoying each other's company without attaching labels, that works for me."

As soon as I heard him spell it out like that, it felt like someone had punched me in the chest. Keeping it casual, keeping it open was what he'd wanted from the start, clearly. He didn't want labels. He just wanted to know if *I* wanted labels.

And did I?

Frankly, I struggled to know what I wanted. Ever. I

hardly ever got more than a glimmer of it when I really tried to figure it out.

And yet, it still hurt to hear that he didn't want anything more serious or exclusive.

Sheesh, what was wrong with me?

At least now I knew asking him to be my boyfriend would probably push him away. I could try to let go of that possibility.

It's not a big deal, Dahlia. Calm down. It's worked out fine so far, hasn't it? Why bother changing it?

Dante and I were just two people enjoying each other's company. How mature of us.

I did my best to put it out of my head. This was fine. Everything was good.

Nothing to overthink at all.

The festival arch appeared, pulling me away from my quiet rumination, and I realized that the sky overhead was now almost entirely a sapphire blue. The last of the clouds were little more than small wisps.

As the crowd of festival goers came into focus, I began recognizing faces in the crowd, and by the time Dante and I passed beneath the archway, folks were calling out to us.

"Dahlia!"

I turned and waved to Fiona Sheehan, the pretty leprechaun who ran Sheehan's Pub. It must be closed for the festival, which made sense. Anyone who wanted a drink among friends could simply come here instead. She gripped a large ceramic stein that sloshed as she waved her arm enthusiastically. The stein looked like one of Raven's, but not like any she made for this year. From a previous year, perhaps. I waved back, happy that she was able to take a day off and let loose. She certainly deserved it with how hard she worked, not only bartending and running the small food service operation the pub had going, but also managing the crowd when the drink made adults act like rowdy children. She was small but fierce.

Dante knew many more people than I did, having grown up in Eastwind. That didn't bother me, because as each new person greeted him, he made sure to ask if they'd already met me, and if not, he introduced me. "This is Dahlia. She works down at Time to Kiln."

Notably, he didn't say, *This is my girlfriend Dahlia.* Because I wasn't that to him.

Gosh, why did it sting so much? Did I want to be his girlfriend? I couldn't be sure. Especially not as I received wave after wave of strong emotions from the crowd of people surrounding me. Was that my joy? My anxiety? My grief? It became impossible to differentiate theirs from mine the longer I experienced it. Thankfully, it wasn't entirely unpleasant. It was, however, quite a ride.

The festival took place on Fluke Mountain, in a large meadow surrounded by tall pines. It was a frequent location for Eastwind festivities, as Dante had explained to me a few days back. One of the biggest attractions, the Lunasa Festival, was held there every year. I'd arrived about three months too late to experience it, but I'd heard it was always a wild time. I looked forward to when it rolled around again at the end of the summer. Would I still be arriving with Dante when that time came?

Atlas stayed so close to me in the crowd that I could feel his body shake slightly against my leg. I didn't mind, though I did feel bad that he was so anxious in the crowd. It was impossible not to feel proud of him for coming with me instead of staying home. He may not have grown less scared of the world than when we'd first met, but he was getting much braver about it. It helped that the word had gotten out that he was not, in fact, a threat, but was rather a big teddy bear with silky-soft fur. Those who might've been afraid of his massive frame and the fearsome reputation of hellhounds instead felt warm and went out of their way to show him kindness. I suspected that those little bits of kindness on a daily basis were what allowed him to be brave. That and the possibility of good scraps once the feast began.

Whatever got him to stay by my side was okay with me, although if he kept getting too many scraps, we might need to find an exercise regimen for him or I would have to roll him to and from the shop each day.

"You doing okay?" I asked him as Dante glad-handed a werebear beside me who I only vaguely recognized.

"No. Not okay at all. Someone could bop me at any minute."

"Yet you decided to come with me today."

"I was told there was a feast," he replied, confirming my suspicion.

"Grim has really rubbed off on you. But I'm glad there's something that's worth being brave for."

"I was told there would be roasted beef."

That was the first I'd heard of it, so clearly Atlas had been gossiping with other familiars or eavesdropping on conversations without my knowledge.

"That does sound delicious," I said.

Eating meat was a whole new experience for me, as a former vegetarian. After coming to Eastwind and learning that none of the meat was actually a product of animal slaughter, I found it easy for me to indulge. And indulge I did. It was impossible not to with all the fantastic cooks in this town!

I waved to Ted as he passed by, the crowd parting to make way for the air of death he carried with him. Mudbug prowled at his heels, completely unseen by most of the festival goers and not appearing to care. The little ghost cat pounced on an ankle, claws out, hissing, then batted at the leather shoelace. The owner of said ankle didn't miss a beat in his conversation with an elf named Siobhan, one of the seven people on the High Council who ran Eastwind.

"You having fun?" Ted asked once he was close enough for us to hear each other over the crowd.

I sighed my relief as his presence brought a calm to my system, blocking out the maelstrom of swirling emotions from the others nearby. "Yes. I'm excited to see all that this has to offer. How did she like the gift?" I asked, nodding down at Buggy.

One could never see Ted's face, as it disappeared beneath the impossible blackness of his hood, but when it came to Ted, I didn't have to see his face to know what expression he was making. His crackling voice captured it perfectly. I could tell he must be smiling as he said, "She went crazy for it! Isn't that right, Buggy? You loved your gift?"

The ghost cat ignored him and batted wildly at a pair of faun hooves passing right by her.

"I think that's why she's so fiery right now. In a good mood from the gift. Or maybe from the blue sky!"

"Blue Sky day is the perfect birthday for her," I replied.

He turned his head toward her, and there was a tender longing in his voice as he said, "It really is, isn't it? She's my blue sky after a long winter."

I felt myself getting choked up. "That's beautiful, Ted."

Buggy took a playful swipe at Atlas, whose hackles went up as he dodged behind me.

"She must be getting restless," he said. "We'll see you around!"

Once the pair had passed through the crowd and out of sight, I scratched Atlas behind the ears. *She's a ghost. She didn't intend you any harm. She knows she can't actually touch you.*

Dante finished up his conversation with the werewolf and took me by the hand. "You okay?" he asked, putting his mouth close to my ear.

I nodded.

"The emotions aren't getting to you?"

"Maybe a little," I conceded, but only because they came crashing down around me in Ted's absence and, yes, it was overwhelming.

He nodded. "Let's get out of the thick of it."

The crowd thinned out around the edges of the meadow, where various games were set up. "This one's my favorite," Dante said, leading me over to it by my hand.

"Oh! I know this one!" I replied excitedly. "Cornhole!"

He arched a brow at me. "What?"

"It's a game we had back home. You throw beanbags and try to get them through the hole on the other board. We call it cornhole. I guess you don't call it that here?"

Before Dante could reply, another voice did. "The rules are a little different."

I turned toward the sound of the voice. Nora and Grim appeared beside us. "It's not far from cornhole," she said, "but the scoring is different. And you use enchanted toad statues." She nodded toward a bucket by the closest board, where large cerulean toads croaked, waiting for their player's next throw. Nora must've seen my concern, because she quickly added, "They're not alive. Think of them as animatronics, but more realistic. No toads are harmed in the making of this game."

I nodded appreciatively, and for a moment my mind went back to the mouse I'd found in the studio earlier that was... dead? Sleeping? I considered about asking Nora what she thought of it but realized it would take too much explaining in a crowded and noisy environment that didn't lend itself to that. I'd ask her later.

"Oh look," Dante said, pointing. "The parade is coming through. That means it's almost time for the feast."

Both Atlas and Grim perked up their ears at the mention of the feast.

The crowd parted just ahead of us, but this time it wasn't for Ted. Instead, I saw Liberty Freeman at the front of a long line of powerful Eastwinders who I'd familiarized myself with out of self-preservation, if nothing else. These were the people in town you didn't want to upset, because they could actually do something about it. It was the High Council leading the way.

While I'd been told that Liberty Freeman was the most powerful person in Eastwind (magically speaking rather than politically—though maybe the two blended together in the end), I never got the sense that he would abuse his power or use it to exact revenge. Every interaction I'd had with him was warm and friendly, and Nora had nothing but good things to say about him. His only weakness, she'd told me, was that he had a poor taste in romantic partners. Apparently, that had come back to haunt almost everyone in town a handful of years before I arrived. She'd started to tell me about it in her kitchen one day, but I never got the full story, because Tanner had arrived home from work just as she was getting started, and she pointedly dropped the subject.

Liberty was a large man. Or, rather, a large genie. (Or maybe an average-size genie? I had no reference point.) His muscular, tanned arms and chest were on full display as he led the procession. His charisma was undeniable. I felt passionate joy flowing off him in waves as he led the parade. Through the crowd, I caught sight of Count Sebastian Malavic, the treasurer of the High Council, and even *he* couldn't resist a smile in response to Liberty's presence. It helped that the genie was shaking his hips, waving to the crowd, and wearing the silliest woven crown of carrot greens atop his bald head.

Behind him, the parade of Eastwind's most notable wore similarly silly garb, all of it related to the winter harvest. Mayor Cordelia Esperia was dressed in a beet-red dress with a hat of green onions. Siobhan had changed since the last time I'd seen her and now wore a necklace of orange, red, and purple carrots around her neck. Darius Pine was dressed like a garlic bulb!

Behind the High Council marched some of the more prominent members of the community. Echo Chambers, a faun who apparently owned half of the businesses in the small but bougie part of Eastwind, wore a knee-length dress covered in fresh herbs. He was perhaps the most fashion-conscious person in all of Eastwind, and every time I passed him around town, he was wearing some new experimental style that drew attention to him and, on the whole, looked rather uncomfortable. Even his dress of herbs seemed like it belonged on a runway somewhere. As he passed, pausing just in front of us to strike a pose and twirl the skirt, I was lucky enough to catch a whiff of his outfit. The smell of rosemary hit first, followed by sage, thyme, and a dozen other vaguely familiar scents swirling in a delicious mélange that made me quietly moan on the inhale.

I locked eyes with Dante, and he was grinning widely. He leaned closer, and said, "That made my stomach growl."

I laughed, "Mine too, now that you mention it."

As the parade came to an end, the crowd filled in behind and followed the procession down a winding forest path to a second meadow where rows and rows of long feast tables awaited.

I was more than happy to allow Dante to pick our seats, and while I was expecting us to end up at a table full of random Eastwinders who I hadn't yet met—and I was okay with that—that's not how it turned out.

"Dante! Dahlia!"

It was Darius Pine, the leader of the werebear clan, who called us over. "I saved you two seats."

Dante didn't hesitate to steer us toward it, but I quickly realized that we were heading toward the *main* table at the center of the festivities and wished we could be anywhere else. I almost said something, but Darius in his garlic bulb costume stood from his seat and waved us over too adamantly to deny him.

"These are for us?" Dante said, gesturing toward the chairs.

"Of course."

"But this is the head table."

Glad I wasn't the only one with questions.

Darius nodded. "Right. The head table is for the High

Council, valued community members, and special guests. I get to choose two special guests. You're them."

Dante looked at me, and I forced a brave smile. "All right, then," Dante said. He pulled out the chair right next to Darius and nodded for me to take it. I tried to act normal around all the bigwigs, beaming and nodding pleasantly in the mood of the occasion.

Once Dante was settled in next to me, Darius leaned toward us and said, "You're doing me a huge favor here. Four of my werebears have been angling for these seats for weeks. Been driving me crazy. They're kissing my hide left and right, making it impossible for me to get any work done. Figured I'd pick the two most low-maintenance people in the sleuth, and that's you two by a mile, so long as Dante doesn't get it in his head to fist-fight anyone."

My sense of pride at being included as one of the werebear sleuth of Eastwind outweighed my self-consciousness, and I was able to settle in more.

"Besides," Darius added, a half-grin breaking through his serious façade, "Dahlia is the newest person in Eastwind. It's nice to get to flex my power a little bit. Maybe you'll be impressed, ditch this guy, and consider dating a real werebear."

Darius enjoyed giving the younger werebears a hard time, so I didn't take him seriously. The mischievous glance he shot Dante told me all I needed to know about his motive, anyway.

"You said you *didn't* want me to get in a fistfight, right?" Dante replied, playfully.

Darius shrugged, leaning back. "Wouldn't be much of a fight. One smack of my paw and you'd be out cold."

"Says a lot that you'd only take me in bear form."

I tuned out from their boyish banter. Darius was like an uncle to Dante, so I wasn't particularly worried about anything escalating. Werebears would be werebears, anyhow.

Perhaps it was the relief and sudden flood of joy everyone felt at seeing the clear sky and bright sun for the first time in months, but not a single person at the head table was anything but kind and warm to me, sharing smiles and hellos. Those who didn't know my name yet asked it and reacted with surprised delight when they matched my name to my face. "Oh yes," said Mayor Esperia, delightedly, "The new Fifth Wind! Welcome! We're glad to have you here! I'll have to introduce you to my friend Serenity. High Priestess. She would love to have you at the next Coven meeting."

Ben Cormac, the leprechaun representative on the High Council gushed, "Eastwind could always use more people with your powers! We had our doubts about Fifth Winds when it was only Ruby, but Nora has certainly opened our eyes to the benefits! Not to mention she introduced queso to the realm!"

The conversation turned to queso for a while after that, as it should, frankly, and only once Liberty Freeman scooted back his chair and got to his feet did the enthusiastic chatter fade out.

"The sky is eternal," he said, his rich voice booming to be easily heard by all. "It was there before me, and it will be there long after I move on. But when the clouds descend, it's easy to believe the blue sky has left us and will never return. Today, we take heart in remembering that it is always there, waiting for us with open arms. The only thing that wavers is our belief that it's still there when we can't see it. When you turn your eyes to the sky, let your faith in its persistence be restored."

Hoots and cheers broke free from his captive audience, and once he asked all the North Wind witches involved in the blue-sky operation to stand and be recognized, the cheers rose even louder.

Liberty's own cheers were perhaps the loudest of all. Two older North Winds at the end of our table were blushing deeply and giggling into their hands until the applause subsided and Liberty continued his speech.

"How many times has our realm faced gray skies? How many times has hope seemed to have abandoned us? How many times have we lost those we loved and felt like the sun would never shine again? Yet it always does. Eventually. This is one of our longest winters of the last two hundred years. I've seen it in the faces of those I pass on the street. The magic of Eastwind is faltering. We are giving up. But not today. And maybe not tomorrow, if we commit ourselves to it. The blue sky is always there, and it is the way we conduct ourselves beneath the cloudy skies, not the clear ones, that defines who we are as a town and as a realm. So, turn your face to the sky. The sun is there. So is the moon. And the stars. They gaze upon us always. Let us remember that, and when we forget, let those here with us today remind us. As long as one person in Eastwind remembers, none of us must forget for long, and the hope of brighter days remains."

He raised his cup for a toast. I reached for mine, expecting it to be empty, but it wasn't. I didn't see anyone come fill the cups, so there was likely culinary magic afoot. Possibly from Liberty himself.

With his cup lifted into the air, he said, "To Eastwind

and all those who dwell within it. To brighter days and blue skies!"

His toast was promptly and enthusiastically seconded by the rest of us. Grinning, he said, "Then, as the host of this year's Blue Sky Festival, I invite you to... dig in!" He snapped his fingers and the tables became filled with heaping bowls and overflowing serving trays of delicious winter harvest.

I was temporarily stunned into silence by the abundance. Dante laughed. "How about we start off simple with a roll?" He held up one with a wreath shape carved into the top of it before setting it on my plate.

"Thanks," I said, snapping out of my surprised state. "This is just... I've never seen something so beautiful."

"The colors really are stunning, aren't they?" He grabbed a gorgeous silver platter. "Glazed carrots?"

"I didn't know carrots came in so many colors," I said.

He chuckled as he dished some onto my plate. "Fair. The Emporium usually only has the red, orange, and purple variety. These blue and teal ones are specially grown by druids up in the higher altitudes of Fluke Mountain. I've only ever seen them at this festival."

Each platter brought a new surprise. Up until that point, I thought I didn't like beets, but when I tried them chopped up in a salad with candied pecans, some sort of soft cheese crumbled over the top, and the unmistakable comfort of rosemary, I quickly changed my stance. The honey-glazed root vegetable might as well have been dessert!

While it had warmed up outside since the sun had emerged, it was still winter, and prior to starting the feast, my body had been well aware of that fact as I hugged my coat closer. But once I started eating, the warm, rich foods made me forget all about the temperature. With the blue sky overhead and my full belly, I might've been laying on a soft blanket by a lake in summer for all the contentedness I felt.

Once the pace of everyone's eating began to slow, Dante leaned in and said, "I just spotted a childhood friend that I haven't seen in a while. I'm gonna go say hello. You're welcome to join, but you can also sit for a little longer and digest. I won't be offended. I can introduce you two later."

Since I was very much enjoying the euphoria of the delicious meal, I nodded. "Sitting here for a bit longer sounds nice."

He disappeared, and a few minutes later, as my brain stopped buzzing with the delicious memory of the rosemary and honey butter on a warm sourdough roll that I'd finished off my meal with, I returned to the present. When I looked around, I realized I was one of only a few still sitting at the table. Across from me, Siobhan Astrid and Ben Cormac were having a lively conversation about the last time they played scufflepuck against each other at Sheehan's Pub, each insisting that they had claimed the victory.

Out of habit, I reached down to pet Atlas, only to realize he wasn't there and it'd been a while since I'd last seen him. He and Grim had taken off together, and while I had a feeling that wouldn't lead to anything *great*—there was no getting around the fact that Grim was a terrible influence on Atlas—I was mostly pleased that Atlas had found such a good friend. I loved having my familiar by my side, but if he could be okay in a crowd without me, that was huge! I was happy for him.

That was, until I looked around and spotted what he and Grim were up to.

I gasped, and my first instinct was to look around, hoping nobody else was seeing what I was.

About twenty yards away, the hellhounds had their front paws up on one of the banquet tables, causing it to bow in the middle under their weight as they tore into the remaining food. Atlas lifted his head, glazed carrots sticking out of his mouth in all directions. A quick flick of his head backward, and he managed to get them all into his slobbery jowls.

I opened my mouth to shout at him, then remembered that I might scare him and set him back weeks of progress with his bravery.

In that way, this brazenness could be considered growth. He was risking quite the surprise bop on the head by indulging so completely in the leftovers.

As calmly as I could, I rose from my seat and wove my way around the tables, through clusters of Eastwinders chatting up one another.

I waited until I was within arm's reach before speaking through the silent, psychic connection. *"Atlas! Grim! What do you two think you're doing?"*

Atlas jerked his head out of a beet pie, but Grim, predictably, answered with, *"Whatever I want,"* and continued lapping from a large cauldron of butternut squash soup.

Atlas dropped his front feet to the ground, hung his head, and tucked his tail between his legs. I felt immediately bad for raising my voice, even if it was only telepathically.

"Everyone was finished," Atlas protested weakly. *"I thought it would be okay."*

Before I could respond, Grim said, *"It's fine. What are they gonna do, try to fight two hellhounds?"*

He had a point. Everyone did seem done with their meal, and it would be a shame to waste food...

"Fine," I said, "but slow down a little. I don't know how to do the Heimlich maneuver on something so big I can't get my arms around it."

Atlas didn't need telling twice; he rejoined Grim with his paws on the table and stuck his head back into the beet pie. His white fur would be stained for days, I was sure.

With that settled (sort of), I looked around for what I should be doing. Without consciously trying, my gaze fell almost immediately on Dante in the crowd. He was talking to a pretty young woman I'd never seen before. They seemed to be enjoying themselves, and as I watched, she laughed and swatted at his arm. He laughed along with her.

What the hellhound? Was that his childhood friend? Had he mentioned it was a woman? No, I was pretty sure I would've noticed. Had he intentionally not mentioned a gender?

I caught myself in the middle of the jealous thought. I didn't like feeling that way at all. And I couldn't remember having felt that way before in my life. This was new. It wasn't me. And besides, he wasn't my boyfriend, so I wasn't entitled to any sort of jealousy about who he talked with. What on earth did I think I could do about it, anyway? March over there and put a stop to it? Yeah, right. Not me. Not in a million years.

You don't want to do that anyway. It's not a big deal. He had friends and a life before you got here. Let it go.

I looked around and spotted a small older woman stacking up plates.

Ooh! Cleaning! Now *there* was something I knew I could help with. Nothing like putting those years of house-cleaning to use.

Cleaning felt comfortable.

"Here, let me help," I said, approaching the leprechaun as she brushed a clump of crumbs off the tablecloth and onto the ground.

"Oh, you don't have to, dear."

"It's okay. I enjoy it."

She assessed me quickly then appeared to believe I meant what I'd said. "Fair enough. Why don't you start down on the end and we'll meet in the middle? I'm just stacking them three tall."

I didn't understand why that was the approach, but I did as she said.

It was nice to have a task to do. I had never felt entirely comfortable with large social gatherings, especially when most of the people were strangers. Dante was a pro at it, but then again, he'd been around Eastwind his whole life and had had time to get to know people more deeply.

Like that pretty young woman...

I shot another glance his way. They were still chatting. Dang it. I'd hoped they'd be done and I could continue convincing myself it was nothing. But it sure looked like *something*.

"You're quite kind," came a voice from beside me.

I jumped and ripped my eyes away from Dante like a guilty child caught in the act.

Liberty Freeman smiled down at me.

"Oh, um... what?" I stammered. Liberty felt like the

closest thing to a celebrity in this town. Having him address me directly felt like someone shining a spotlight on me.

He grinned. "You're quite kind, I said. All these festivities available, all these people to talk to, and you're choosing to clean the tables."

I forced myself to blink. I probably looked like a deer in the headlights. Or maybe a weredeer in the headlights, considering. "I don't know about *kind*. It's more like somebody needs to clean, right?"

He simply arched an eyebrow at me. "You're right. But you don't have the magic to make it easy."

"Neither does she," I said, nodding toward the leprechaun.

Liberty chuckled. "No, she just does this every year. I keep telling her it's not necessary, but she won't listen. I suspect she enjoys it. To each their own." He paused, and I watched with embarrassment as his attention turned to where mine had just been: Dante. "Planning on intervening there?"

I felt my cheeks redden. "What? No. He can talk to whoever he wants."

"I thought you two were together." Liberty grinned slyly.

"No. I mean, we kind of are, but it's not..." I sighed. He didn't need me to finish the thought, and the two of us watched the ongoing conversation. Dante said something, and the pretty woman covered her mouth with her hands as she threw her head back and laughed. What in the hellhound could they be talking about that could be so funny? And then she leaned forward and placed a hand on his bicep. The same bicep he'd offered me as we walked to the festival together. I blinked away the unfamiliar emotions welling up inside me.

"He can do what he wants," I said, though I wasn't sure who I was trying to convince exactly.

Liberty raised his chin slightly, inspecting me down his strong nose. "What about what *you* want?"

"It doesn't matter. It's not worth getting all worked up about."

He chuckled and held up his hands in mimed surrender. "Whatever you say. But, speaking as someone who's dated his fair share of truly jealous women, it doesn't always bother someone to know that the person they're interested in has some firm boundaries and some hard lines not to be crossed."

I sighed, my shoulders feeling suddenly heavy. "I wouldn't even know where to draw a hard line." I wasn't sure why I was suddenly confiding all this to a person I hardly knew, but something about Liberty told me he could keep a secret and was probably kind enough not to judge me.

"Knowing what you want and don't want is just a matter of practice." He snapped his fingers and all the plates and food disappeared, leaving only clean table cloths and the winter harvest centerpieces behind.

I gasped and took a half step back. You'd think that I would've gotten used to seeing such blatant signs of magic after living here for months, but that wasn't the case.

A growl behind me got my attention, and I saw Grim staring down at the now empty table, his hackles raised, teeth bared. Atlas cowered beneath the table, no doubt frightened by the sudden change.

I turned back to Liberty, who was grinning. "Drawing

hard lines can be quite useful. For instance, I just saved you a long night of letting your familiar in and out of the house due to an upset stomach."

Had he been watching me talk to Atlas and Grim? Did he somehow know how our conversation had gone? It sure seemed like he did.

And he knew I hadn't been able to tell them 'no', either.

" 'No' can be a kindness," he said.

I stared down at my feet, hugging my coat tighter to me. "I mean, you're right. It's never been easy for me to say, though. For one, I'm sometimes the last to know what I want. But I'm slow to figure it out, and by then, someone's usually already walked all over me."

"You've got to stand up for yourself," he said.

"I wish I knew how."

"Do you?"

"Absolutely. But I have to know what I want before I can do that. I just... when the moment comes, when someone asks me what I want, it's impossible. I would have an easier time swimming in quicksand. My brain freezes. Everyone acts like knowing what you want is simple, but I don't find it simple at all."

Liberty gently rested a massive hand on my shoulder. "Hey, cheer up. You're young. There's still plenty of time to learn. Where there's a wish, there's a way." He squeezed my shoulder gently then let his hand fall back to his side. "Why don't you practice by going and joining the conversation with Dante and his old friend?"

"Do you... do you know her?"

He nodded. "I do. Lovely werebear, I won't deny it. Fun, friendly, kind."

"Are you trying to hurt my feelings?" I asked.

He chuckled. "Not at all. But maybe I *am* trying to light a little fire under your hide."

"Thanks, but that doesn't work for me." I pulled my eyes away from Dante and the woman. "I think I'll just walk home instead."

Liberty appeared supremely disappointed in my decision, and, well, I couldn't blame him. But it was probably nothing, right? Just an old friend. Nothing to get fired up about. Far be it from me to interrupt a lively chat between long-time friends.

I called out to Atlas through our connection and let him know we were heading out. Now that food scraps were off the table, literally, he didn't seem bothered by the idea of escaping the crowd.

I imagined someone like Nora or perhaps even Grace would have no problem walking right up to their significant other and interrupting his conversation with some pretty lady they didn't know. And that was partly why I admired them so much.

To be fair, I consoled myself, *Dante isn't your significant other. He gave you that opportunity today and you didn't take it. If you hope to keep him around at all, you can't start smothering him.*

"*Why are we leaving so soon?*" Atlas asked as we entered the trail through the woods toward the festival grounds. "*Something dangerous about to happen?*"

"No, *nothing like that. I'm just ready to be home, aren't you?*"

"*It does sound nice. Maybe we can creep in quietly to avoid waking the beast.*"

I ran my fingers through his thick fur. "You're still afraid of that little munchkin cat?"

"It's smart to be afraid of her. She's deadly and criminally insane."

I wasn't sure I entirely agreed. Atlas was easily ten times Monster's size, and while she did like to pounce on him from hiding places throughout Nora and Tanner's home, she hadn't left any scratches on him that I'd ever seen. "If we do wake her, she'll take one look at those red stains all over your muzzle and run the other way."

He licked his chops. "We'll see. Let's not tempt it, though. Going unnoticed is the only way to stay safe."

While that wasn't an unusual creed to hear from him, hearing it right as I snuck away from a big festival unnoticed because I was too scared to interrupt Dante's conversation with a pretty girl made his declaration feel uncomfortably personal.

He couldn't have known, though, so I gave him a scratch behind the ears and said, "We'll be as quiet as we can. And maybe we can try to get some of that beet juice out of your fur once we're safely in our room."

CHAPTER FOUR

As I walked to work the following morning beneath a dark, pre-dawn sky, I was accompanied not only by Atlas, but by a nebulous cloud of guilt from the previous day. Dante had sent me an owl before I'd managed to fall asleep, checking on me. He'd assumed that I'd left the festival so early and without letting him know because something was terribly wrong. His short message asked if I'd had an upset stomach or if Atlas wasn't feeling well. It also asked if he could help with whatever it was.

I hadn't slept particularly well, but I'd slept soundly enough to wake up with a clearer head. And my clear head told me quite pointedly that I'd overreacted. Dante cared about me, clearly. And Atlas too. All he'd done was talk to another woman, an old friend, no less, and I'd picked up and left?

I couldn't stand to think too hard about it, so I shoved it all as quickly as I could from my head. The result was that the vague cloud of guilt hovering around me and clinging to my skin was only made worse by the fact that I hadn't yet responded to his message. What would I even say?

I was ready to arrive at the studio and distract myself by getting ready for my shift. I didn't anticipate just how quickly I would be offered up a major distraction.

I unlocked the back door to the studio, flipped on the lights, and took a few steps inside, not much looking where I was going, until...

"Oh goodness!" I jumped backward.

Atlas yelped and ran behind a rack of dry greenware.

I blinked down at the thing on the floor that had spooked me. Another mouse lay motionless, right in my path. Like the one the day before, which had laid in nearly the same spot on the floor, this one could've been mistaken for simply being asleep. It looked still as death, too, just like the other. The other that had turned out to be alive enough to scamper off.

My initial shock quickly gave way to curiosity. Why was this mouse here, in the same spot as yesterday's? It didn't make any sense.

I looked above me to see if there was anything on the ceiling that could explain it—an air duct or even some sort of curse scribbled that might explain the fate of rodents that pass beneath it. Nothing of note, though. It looked like every other part of the ceiling. Had someone left the mice for me to find?

A chill ran down my spine. I didn't like that possibility at all.

And, oh, the poor little thing.

I crouched down next to him to get a closer look. His little chest wasn't moving up and down at all that I could see. His mouth was open, and his tiny tongue lolled out.

Maybe the one yesterday had merely been sleeping, but this one had clearly expired. "Sweet tiny mouse," I said, feeling my heart break for it.

I grabbed a small rag and returned to pick it up, just like I'd done the day before. I reached down and scooped him up as gently as possible. It deserved a little burial, at the very least, even if that made me a few minutes late opening up the shop. I couldn't stand seeing such a small, frail creature this way. What had happened to it? Had the little mouse known it was about to die? Had it thought about all its little mousey friends who would miss it?

I was overwhelmed by sadness for this little critter. I wanted him not to be dead, and I wanted it with all my heart...

Its back leg twitched. Its head shot up, and our eyes met. We blinked at each other for a moment before it popped up and leaped out of my hands, scurrying across the floor and disappearing behind a shelf of plaster molds.

Déjà vu. But I had been *so sure* the mouse was dead this time! And then suddenly, it was very clearly not dead. It had opened his eyes and looked at me. Could both things have been true? Could it have been dead and not dead? Could I have somehow managed to...

No, I didn't like that thought, *at all*. Ruby had once alluded to that power of the Fifth Wind before. I hadn't liked the sound of it then, and I didn't like it now.

I hadn't *tried* to conjure any magic with the mouse, not the one today or the one yesterday. Did my intention matter? Had I accidentally...?

I shoved the idea from my mind and vowed never to so much as suggest it to Atlas, who might never sleep again if I did.

"Is it gone?" he asked from his hiding place.

"Yes, I got rid of it." Sort of. It mostly got rid of itself.

He poked out his snout to sniff the air. It was still stained pink from yesterday's beet pie.

"Why was it there?"

"No idea, Atlas."

There I was, yet again, desperate for a distraction from worrisome thoughts, from questions I'd rather not ask, in case I didn't like the answer.

I continued on with my morning as best I could, prepping the studio for the early classes before flipping the shop sign from closed to open. The place probably didn't need a dusting for another couple of days, but I decided to go ahead and grab the feather duster anyway. There were so many delicate pieces around the shop that it required my full attention to dust effectively while making sure I didn't knock anything over. It always required my attention.

I was grateful when customers began showing up toward the end of my self-imposed chore, because it meant I could continue to avoid thinking about the mouse and Dante for a while longer. The morning rush appeared to be fueled by commonplace envy. Eastwinders arrived at the shop to secure themselves one of our remaining stock of Raven's steins, having seen so many of the beautiful pieces at the festival. I was happy to help them out, and I couldn't wait for Raven to see how much of the inventory I'd moved along.

Raven dropped in around lunchtime and she'd brought me a warm coffee, which was kind of her. Her dark purple hair was tied back in a knot, exposing the definition of her jaw and cheekbones. She was a South Wind, perhaps in her late fifties, though I'd never been rude enough to ask her age, and you could tell she'd lived her life exactly as she wanted by the sharpness of her eyes and the quickness of her mind.

"I don't know about you," she said, leaning a hip against the shop counter and sipping her own cup of coffee, "but Jude and I stayed out too late last night. We always do that on Blue Sky Day. The little bit of optimism goes a long way toward making it impossible to call an end to the party. Well, you know how it goes. I noticed you at Sheehan's even as Jude and I were heading out." She winked at me. "Figured you'd need a midday caffeine break like I do."

I paused mid-sip, lowering the cup. "Oh. I mean, I am a little tired, but I wasn't at Sheehan's last night."

Raven's brows pinched together. "What do you mean? I saw you there. You were playing scufflepuck with Ted."

I shook my head, pouting out my lips. "No. I wasn't there. Maybe it was someone who looks like me?"

She arched a dubious brow at me. "I *suppose*, but I don't know of anyone in Eastwind who looks like you. You sure you weren't there? Listen, I'm not your mother. As long as you get here on time, I don't care if you're hungover."

I chuckled. "It wasn't me, Raven. I don't know what to tell you."

She shrugged. "Okay, fine, maybe I drank more than I thought. Or maybe I just dreamed that. Either way, coffee never hurts."

I could tell from the taste that it wasn't Medium Rare coffee. But then again, why would it be? The diner was about a fifteen-minute walk from the studio, and Raven and Jude lived together in a little house right behind the studio.

That would be out of her way. "Mmm..." I held it up. "Did you brew this at home?"

Raven smiled. "I wish I knew how to make that at home. It's a honey lavender latte from Necro Coffee."

I knew of the place, over in the shopping district. Mostly I knew it from Nora not appreciating the name. Apparently, years before I'd arrived in town, necromancers like me weren't treated with much respect. Necro Coffee's slogan was, *Coffee so good it'll raise the dead.* Clever, I know. It didn't particularly bother me, but then again, I'd only ever been treated with mild suspicion for being a Fifth Wind witch. Nora and Ruby had done the hard work of changing the town's opinion of Fifth Winds from one of open contempt to simmering distrust. I owed them big time for that.

The mention of Necro Coffee and their slogan brought my mind back to one of the things I'd spent so much effort not thinking about this morning. "Hey, Raven, I thought I should mention that I've been finding... dead mice in the studio. One yesterday, one today. I don't really know what to make of it."

Raven shrugged. "Maybe nothing to make of it at all. They probably got into some of the glaze powders."

I'd suspected as much, and I was glad to hear someone knowledgeable agree.

She went on, "At least they're dead and that's two fewer mice to chew through drums and bins."

While I didn't share her animosity toward the mice, and I certainly wasn't going to tell her that neither had *stayed* dead, I still felt better having brought it up.

Not only had the conversation with Raven helped ease my mind, but the caffeine had pulled me out of my shame fog, and I decided I ought to be a little bit more proactive and set things right with Dante. I didn't want him worrying that I was mad at him. I wasn't. Not *really*. I was maybe a little insecure, but not angry.

He could talk to whomever he chose to. Of course he had lots of friends. He was a nice man and a good friend to many. Some of those friends would happen to be pretty werebears, just by the odds...

I used the lull of customers as an opportunity to grab a piece of parchment and write out a note to him:

Sorry about leaving suddenly. Was tired and crashed out early. Atlas had a rough night too. We woke up and went straight to work this morning. Dinner tonight?

I rolled up the parchment and sent it off with an owl that had been snoozing on the perch outside the front door of the shop. It hadn't seemed too perturbed by being woken up, so I hoped that meant it would deliver my message without delay. The owls of Eastwind had a strong reputation for reliability when it came to the post. I had a sense that they were one of those systems that functioned so dependably that nobody ever thought about it unless something went terribly wrong.

When I returned inside, I was feeling much better about myself. Not only had I found a way to respond without lying too much about the reason I'd left, but I'd just asked him out to dinner. How bold!

Maybe the boldness could carry over into dinner, and I could reopen the conversation he'd started yesterday. Maybe I could tell him that I *would* be okay with being his girlfriend. Did I want that? I suspected I did, though I couldn't be entirely sure. It could be fun to call him my boyfriend. And then maybe he would get the message that he didn't need to be talking to pretty women I didn't know...

Oh, come on, Dahlia. It's not that big a deal. Let it go.

An owl returned not long after with a response. It grabbed the clapper of the mail bell in its beak and shook it to notify me of a message. When I opened the small slip of parchment from Dante and read his response, the pinching of jealousy in my gut struck swiftly:

Sounds great. I had plans to grab something with Izzy tonight and catch up (she's been away at art school in Avalon for the last year), but you're obviously welcome to join. I think you'd like her. Franco's Pizza at 7?

So, the woman had a name. Izzy. I disliked her already.

You don't know her, a little voice in my head warned. *If Dante likes her, she's probably okay.*

But despite my attempt to calm down, another part of me replied with, *He liked Lydia too, and she killed Frida Dune and tried to kill you, too.*

From his place by my feet beneath the shop's counter, Atlas said, *"Lydia killed because she was jealous. You really want to go down that path?"*

I glared at him. "Stop eavesdropping on my private thoughts."

"Stop thinking so loud I can't block it out."

It wasn't like him to sass me—I could also blame his newfound snark on Grim's influence, surely—but the shock of his mouthiness did succeed in pulling me out of my dark and pointy thoughts.

He was right anyway. Lydia had tried to kill me because she thought—correctly, as it turned out—that her ex-boyfriend was showing interest in me. Jealousy had driven her to murder.

I had no intention of killing Izzy, or even saying an unkind word to her, but still. Jealousy was a road best not taken. Lydia probably didn't set out intending to kill anyone when she first fanned the flames of that emotion. But things happen if we're not careful.

Fine. I would go have dinner with Dante and meet his friend Izzy. Maybe she would be wonderful and kind and clearly have no interest in him. Maybe we would get along really well and I'd have a new friend in town for as long as she stayed. If I could keep my head on straight and contain my baser impulses, this might work out well for everyone.

I responded to his message with a confirmation that I would meet him there.

And then I put it out of my mind for the rest of the workday.

Mostly.

CHAPTER FIVE

I could've found Franco's Pizza with my eyes closed, not because I'd been there that many times since coming to Eastwind, but because as soon as I reached the Emporium, the delicious scent of pizza, pasta with roasted tomatoes, and warm focaccia bread met my nostrils, causing me to momentarily close my eyes in pleasure. I could have found my way by smell from there on.

Atlas followed close at my heels. He had spent the day looking forward to some complimentary meatballs, which the owner, Jane Saxon, always supplied when one of the town's three hellhounds dropped by. Nobody had a softer spot for hellhounds than werewolves and werebears, apparently.

I also suspected that Atlas was accompanying me in a novel protective role, which suited him well. But his bulk and fearsome red eyes wouldn't be needed, because we both knew that the protection I might need was from myself and my own potentially disastrous emotions. If that jealousy reared its head again, Atlas might hear it and talk some sense into me before I could make a mess of things. I appreciated that even as I somewhat resented it.

I arrived right at seven on the dot, expecting to be the first at the restaurant. But when I reached the host stand and opened my mouth to ask for a table for three, my wandering eyes landed right on Dante.

And Izzy.

They were already there. Seated and with a drink in front of each.

How long had they been here, just the two of them chatting quietly by candlelight? Had he given me the wrong time on purpose?

It was a silly thought. I had no reason to suspect Dante of lying. He was terminally honest. His sense of integrity was one of the things I liked most about him. It wasn't fair to assume the worst of him, and assuming the worst of people wasn't like me at all. Sheesh, I was suddenly acting batty about this whole relationship.

And, lest I forget, Dante liked me. He told me that. He made me a teapot for Winter Solstice. And the kissing was probably a hint as well.

"Ah, they're already here," I said to the host, a petite faun, as I pointed toward the table.

Izzy had her back to me, so Dante was the first to spot Atlas and me approaching. As he did, his eyes lit up. He grinned and stood from his seat.

Yes, I was just being dumb. This guy liked me. I needed to stop making up scenarios in my head.

"Izzy, this is Dahlia!"

Izzy stood from her seat across from him and opened her arms for a hug. "So nice to meet you!"

I wasn't sure yet that I wanted to hug her, but doing so

was easier than not, so I went in. She was tall and thin, but the hug was warm and pleasant, not at all one of those timid hugs with the shoulders slumped forward.

Dang it, I might just like her yet!

Dante leaned forward and gave me a quick kiss on the cheek before I took a seat at a chair on the side of the table between them.

"And who is this?" Izzy said, smart enough not to try to pet someone's familiar without asking.

"Atlas," I said. "He's just here for the meatballs."

Izzy laughed and it had the delightful timber of a wind-chime. "Same, Atlas. The meatballs are to die for."

"Is that a threat?" he said, flattening his ears against his head and ducking behind my chair.

"No, just a figure of speech," I assured him. *"Don't worry."*

"I hope you don't mind," Dante said, holding up a wine glass. "We went ahead and got started on drinks."

"Not at all," I said, my attention drifting from Izzy's glass of white wine to the bottle of it on the center of the table. "Am I running late? I thought you said seven."

He waved away my concern. "Not running late, don't worry. Izzy didn't have anything pressing to do today, so she was killing time at the bar. It's been a slow day, so Jane cut me early. Figured we might as well get started." He held up his wine glass.

"Oh. Cool." A totally plausible explanation. Jane, who owned Franco's Pizza, was a considerate boss as well as Dante's aunt by marriage. It sounded just like her to cut him early so he could spend time with a friend.

I turned to Izzy. "Dante said you're in town from Avalon, right?"

"Yes! Well, I used to live here. I don't know how much Dante has told you about me." She cast him a quick questioning look and waited for him to jump in.

"Oh, uh. Nothing, really," he said.

She chuckled. "Really? I thought you two spent a lot of time together at the pottery studio. And you never mentioned me? Okay, then. I'll try not to get my feelings hurt." She seemed to just be playfully needling him, but I felt that strange tickle that something was off here. Fortunately, I was getting quicker at pushing it to the back of my mind.

"We went to school together," she continued. "I stuck around Eastwind as long as I could, and I do love this place and my clan, but... Some people are just built for a metropolis. My family took a vacation to Wisconsin when I was younger. Dante's probably told you about it. The realm is a big vacation spot for weres. Lots of dense forest to roam around in, no witches to—" She caught herself. "I'm sorry. I'm not prejudiced against witches. It's just that... when I was growing up here, a lot of them looked down on the werebears and all the other weres. There was still a lot of prejudice against us. I know a lot of witches now who are wonderful, though! You seem lovely too, from everything Dante's told me."

Unsure what she wanted me to say to all that, I flashed her a reassuring smile, which I wasn't quite feeling.

"Anyway, we went to Wisconsin, but you can't get there directly from Eastwind. You have to go through Avalon, which is a hub realm. A lot of realms branch off from it, including Eastwind and Wisconsin. We were only in Avalon for a few hours, but I just *knew* it was where I belonged. So as soon as I saved up enough money working as a stylist at Echo's Salon, I applied to the Avalonian Art Institute. And I got in!"

"Wow," I said, knowing not a single thing about the application process but sensing that it was my cue to be impressed. "Congratulations."

Dante leaned forward. "You should see her sculptures. Incredible."

"You can show her," Izzy prompted, grinning.

"Oh right!" Dante replied. "She brought me one to keep. It's in my apartment."

I looked back and forth between them. "You brought him a sculpture. How... nice."

Beneath the table, Atlas nipped me on the ankle.

I got the message and took a deep breath.

Jane Saxon undoubtedly had all kinds of other things to do around the restaurant, but she came and waited on us herself anyway. She arrived with a plate of meatballs already in hand and set them on the floor for Atlas before rolling her shoulders back and taking in the three of us at the table.

It was a moment before she seemed to know what to make of it and flashed a smile. "Dahlia, how about we start with you. What are you in the mood for tonight?"

As we went around the table to order, I felt supremely grateful for Jane's presence. The way she seemed to size up the situation and see that something about it seemed off made me feel a little less crazy.

Not only was Jane married to Dante's uncle Ansel, but she was Nora's best friend. And no doubt owning a restaurant so close to the center of town meant she kept up to date on all the town gossip. I wondered what she might know about Dante and Izzy's relationship that I didn't.

After we each ordered our dinner, Jane cast one last look at the three of us and then smiled and said our food would be right out.

"So, Dahlia," Izzy said, "where did you live before Eastwind?"

Dante beat me to it. "I haven't told you? She's from New Orleans!"

Izzy waited expectantly for him to go on, and when he didn't, she turned politely toward me and said, "New Orleans?"

I opened my mouth to reply that it was fine if she hadn't heard of it, but Dante jumped in again.

"That's where Eva ended up."

Izzy's brows pinched together. "Eva Moody?"

I looked back and forth between them, trying to figure out what was happening behind this conversation.

Evangeline Moody, known around here as Eva, was a South Wind witch who had mostly lived up in one of Darius Pine's cabins for the short time she was in Eastwind. As a result, she was well-known within the clan, and, from what Dante had told me, beloved.

But then something had happened—I'd never gotten the full story on it—but Eva had ended up back in New Orleans where she opened The South Wind, a magic store I had frequented before I died and came to Eastwind. I knew her as Angelina.

I had so many questions I wished I could've asked her before I came here, but of course I had no idea I would cross over realms.

Or even that there were different realms.

I knew that Dante had been a fan of Eva—I suspected it helped that she was beautiful and single on and off while she was here, though she had years on him so I didn't guess they'd ever dated—but I had no idea how Izzy felt about her. I also had no idea if learning that I came from the same place would change her opinion on me, whatever that was at this point.

"Yeah, Eva Moody. Dahlia comes from the same place," Dante continued. "She even knows her."

Izzy's mouth fell open as she turned to me. "No way."

"Yep," I said.

I couldn't fully read her expression as she continued to gape at me. "Do you plan on staying here or going back eventually?" she asked.

I blinked. "I, uh, I don't know. I guess it never occurred to me that I could just... go back." I turned to Dante. "But if Eva did it, then I suppose there's a way."

Dante shrugged. "I don't know how she did it. If anyone else does, they're not talking. He paused. "Wait, would you *want* to go back?"

"No," I said, and the speed with which I said it was a surprise to even myself. "I like it better here."

Dante smiled, and I hoped that meant he was glad I would stay.

The topic had me feeling squeamish in a way I didn't fully understand, so I said to Izzy, "How long are you visiting?"

She brushed off the question quickly with, "Not sure yet. Maybe a couple of days. I don't need to go back to Avalon for a few weeks." Then she turned to Dante and said, "You remember that time Florence Dormant accidentally shifted in the middle of math class?"

Dante threw his head back and laughed. I forced a grin and a gentle chuckle, but not too big of one. It was a thin line to walk—look like you're enjoying yourself while accepting that you have no idea what the other people are talking about and have essentially been cut out of the conversation.

The story of Florence's misfortune quickly spun into a sequence of stories from their years of friendship and growing up together, none of which I had any involvement in.

"Do they even want me here?" I asked Atlas forlornly, after half an hour without having so much as a single word to contribute to their reminiscing.

He didn't respond. I jabbed him with my toe to see if he'd fallen asleep.

"I don't know what you want me to say," he replied.

"Tell me I'm wrong."

"You want me to lie?"

I sighed. I didn't want him to lie. I simply didn't want to be the third wheel here, but it was clear enough that I was.

"You could interrupt them," Atlas suggested. *"Turn the conversation to something else."*

"Like what?" Honestly, my mind was coming up short. *"It's probably best for everyone if I give them their space."*

The first opportunity I got, I placed a few coins on the table to cover my meal and said, "I'd better get going. I have to open the shop again in the morning."

Dante seemed to snap out of a shared reverie with Izzy, and he said, "Huh? Oh. Okay."

Without another word to either of them, I followed Atlas out of the restaurant without looking back.

CHAPTER SIX

There was a fresh dusting of snow on the ground the next morning as I made my way from the warm comfort of Nora and Tanner's house through the quiet streets of Eastwind on my way to Time to Kiln.

Atlas had opted to sleep in, which I couldn't really blame him for. While the thought of staying bundled up under my covers with the warm body of a large hellhound snoozing at my feet sounded delectable, I could also enjoy it vicariously, knowing he was able to stay warm and cozy a bit longer. Meanwhile, I had a job that I very much wanted to keep.

The sun wouldn't rise for another half hour as I strolled down the cobblestone streets through town. This was a familiar route now, I realized with some satisfaction. I was settling into life here.

I'd never experienced a dark sky like this back in New Orleans. For one, I didn't usually leave the house at night if I could help it, and during those late jobs where I couldn't avoid it—the final night of my life came to mind—I tried to stick to well-lit paths for safety purposes.

The darkness here was different, though. It was quiet. Peaceful. Despite the occasional murder in this town, I didn't feel on edge walking around alone. The darkness didn't feel so much like a threat or an accomplice in crime, but rather what is was—a natural part of the environment.

My eyes had no problem adjusting to the dark. I wasn't sure if that was a result of my body settling into its new home or some power associated with being a Fifth Wind that I had yet to learn about. The light snowfall was enough to dampen the sounds around me, so all I heard was the occasional hoot of an owl and the snow crunching beneath my boots.

I turned onto a wide street, off which was Time to Kiln. Along the wider road were small, floating balls of light every twenty or so yards, glowing brightly enough to guide my way but not so bright that it interrupted my night vision.

I hadn't encountered anyone on my walk through the neighborhood streets along my route, but when I emerged onto the main street that branched out from Fulcrum Park like the spoke of a wheel, there were a handful of other folks setting up for the day. A fruit vendor tended to her cart, pulling back the covering and, with a flick of her wand, conjuring a sign for her business that hovered above the cart. One more flick, and the lettering of the sign began to glow in the darkness: *Unmagicked Fruit.*

I didn't know her name, but we'd passed each other frequently enough in the mornings that I waved and she waved back.

I recognized nearly everyone along this route, now. We

were a fellowship of the early risers, and while we might not be fully awake as we passed one another, it brightened my day to simply say hello and have someone return the gesture.

It was my growing familiarity with the usuals along my route that made the stranger I spotted up ahead stand out to me. She was heading in the same direction I was, so she had her back to me, but I could tell she was roughly my height and must've shared my style taste, because she was wearing an identical deep purple coat to the one I had on.

She passed beneath the floating lights as she walked with a clear purpose, and when the next splash of light fell upon her, I couldn't help but notice her thick, dark, curly hair flowing from beneath her wool cap. The hair caught my attention mostly because it seemed so familiar. In fact, it looked a heck of a lot like mine.

Who was she? I wondered. A new Eastwinder? A vacationer from Avalon? She would have to be, because while I didn't know everyone in town yet, I was pretty sure I'd at least *seen* most of the people at things like the Blue Sky Festival or shopping at the Eastwind Emporium. I would've noticed a woman about my height with the same hair.

Time to Kiln appeared up ahead, and the curious side of me was disappointed that I wouldn't be able to catch up to her and solve this little mystery of her identity.

But then she turned toward Time to Kiln, too.

She didn't approach the front of the shop, cup a hand against the window, and try to peer through, which I had subconsciously expected her to do. Instead, she turned off the street on the other side of the building and went around toward the back, disappearing between Time to Kiln and the crystal store next to it.

What the heck?

Curiosity caused me to pick up the pace. Despite the teapot wrapped carefully in a cloth inside my canvas bag that I very much didn't want to rattle around too much (I had plans for the teapot later), I was close to a jog by the time I reached where she'd veered off the street. I squinted down at the ground and picked out the slight impression of boot prints in the thin white layer of snow on the grass between the shops. As quietly as I could, I followed the trail.

It led to the back door of the studio.

I looked around. No lights were on in Raven and Jude's house behind the studio. They preferred to sleep in, hence hiring me or Sasha to open each day, so no surprise there. No sign of the woman I'd followed back here, though.

Briefly, I wished Atlas was with me before remembering that he would've already skidoo-ed from the situation by now.

I tried the back door to the studio, and with relief, discovered that it was locked. When I looked down again, I noticed that the boot prints had led up to the door, yes, but then they led away again, around the other side of the building.

It was clear that whoever she was, she'd tried to get into the studio through the back door but had thankfully found it locked.

I mustered some courage and jogged after the prints around the other side of the building, hoping to get a better look at her. Too slow. When I emerged onto the street again and looked around, I didn't see anyone with my coat.

Who was she? Why had she tried to get into the studio? And why did she have such good taste in coats?

It was all so strange. Could she have anything to do with the mice I'd found?

As badly as my brain demanded answers to the many questions, I shrugged them off as likely unsolvable with the limited information I had. Not to say my mind completely let go of the questions, but I did my best to go about my business as usual and not let them derail me. I was already doing so well this morning about not thinking too much on dinner with Dante and Izzy the night before, and I wanted to keep that streak of tuning out from my thoughts going.

I unlocked the back door of the studio and stepped inside, out of the cold.

It was studio policy to keep the back door locked when nobody was working in the studio, but it was *unofficial* policy that nobody cared and the studio was more of a communal space for those who took lessons or visited during open studio hours than anything privately owned. There was even a co-op that Raven and Jude offered, which was essentially a monthly membership to come in whenever you liked and use the facilities as you pleased.

This morning, I went with the official policy and locked the door behind me.

Trying not to let my imagination get the best of me, I hummed a tune that I'd learned as a child, one that was often played in the streets of my neighborhood. It worked so well to calm my nerves that I almost didn't notice the snake on the ground until my foot was two inches from stepping right down on it.

I yelped, jumped back, and bumped into the shelf of drying greenware, which I had to scramble to steady again. I returned my attention quickly to the snake and discovered that it hadn't moved an inch. Either it was an overconfident snake that didn't think anyone would dream of stepping on it, or it was no longer alive.

Oh gosh, not this again.

It wasn't a big snake, thankfully. It was lying in an S-shape, but stretched out it might be a couple of feet from tail to head. And it was pencil thin. Likely a garter snake or something similar. I admit, I wasn't well versed on the fauna and flora of Eastwind. The wildlife had so much wilderness to enjoy outside the main parts of town that it generally stayed out there and didn't need to risk coming into contact with magical beings.

I had not a single clue if this snake was venomous or not. Or, frankly, if it was even a normal snake and not something like a... weresnake? Did those exist? I had no idea.

I checked the clock on the wall. No one else would be in for likely another hour and a half. I wasn't a huge fan of snakes. Most of the ones I'd encountered in New Orleans had jumped out at me out of nowhere, from beneath a pile of junk on a patio or camouflaged in dead leaves. My approach had always been to move in the opposite direction from it and continue to give it as much space as possible until one of us died of old age.

Judging simply by sight, the snake on the floor now had reached that finish line. Did I let it sit there, or did I have to clean it up?

But then I remembered the mice I'd encountered and the dignity I'd attempted to give them by moving them back outside into nature. Granted, neither one had turned out to actually be dead—or maybe they were and I really, *really* needed to talk to Nora about some of my powers—but it didn't seem fair to not at least try to offer the same to the snake. It couldn't help being a snake, just like I couldn't help being a witch. And something had, it seemed, killed it. Could it have gotten into a glaze, as Raven had suggested for the mice? It was possible.

I grabbed a towel from the spare stack and doubled it over. Then, to be sure, I doubled it over again. If this thing *wasn't* dead, and if it was venomous, I wouldn't regret having extra material between its fangs and my hand.

I bent down and lifted the little rope of a thing from the ground. It was already stiff and reminded me of a dry pasta noodle. I laid it down the length of my towel-draped arm.

It was actually quite cute, when I paused to look at it. And frail. Poor thing. There I was, fearing it, yet it was so little and too small to survive. Weren't we all just creatures trying to make our way in the world?

I carried it to the back door and stepped outside with it. The cold wind felt harsher than before.

Kneeling beneath a young tree, I looked down at the little S-shaped body. "Rest in peace, little thing. I don't know how you died, but I'm sorry you did." My caution gave way to compassion, and I dragged a finger down the smooth scales of the snake's back.

I should've known better, truly. Because not a second after I did so, the snake started wiggling.

"Siren's song!" I said, borrowing a phrase from the locals as I fell back onto my rear end.

The snake slithered off the towel and onto the frosty ground, where it quickly disappeared into the shadows.

I scrambled to my feet and wiped the snow off the back of my coat and pants. "What the...?"

A quick check around me to make sure no one saw that,

and then I scrambled back inside and locked the door behind me.

The snake had been in roughly the same spot as the mice I'd found previously. Was someone leaving the dead critters there for me to find? And if so, who?

My mind immediately jumped back to the woman in the matching coat. Could she have a key to the studio that I didn't know about? Could she have gotten in and out fast enough to leave me a dead snake?

And more importantly, why would she? Why would anyone?

The questions offered me no immediate answers, but they haunted me all the same.

CHAPTER SEVEN

The day quickly swept me up into it, and I only wondered about the snake and the mice in the few lulls between helping customers. The shop often went hours between customers, which was what had allowed Raven and Jude to go so long before hiring a clerk to stay up front. But it seemed that the Blue Sky Festival had put a shopping bug in everyone that was lasting for days. A little bit of envy could do that. Raven had anticipated as much, and thankfully she'd made plenty of gorgeous stoneware tankards for those who wanted one just like what they'd seen others drinking from at the festival.

And while customers were already there... they may as well pick up something else, right? That seemed to be the sentiment, at least.

Everyone seemed to need a new teapot or a mortar and pestle or an enchanted serving dish to bundle with their new tankard. Even the little spoon rests that Grace liked to hand build as she waited for her wheel-thrown pieces to dry to leather hard sold like crazy. Granted, the spoon rests were undeniably beautiful, with hand-painted scenes of meadows or mountains over a pearly white background. I'm sure it didn't hurt that she'd also added a self-cleaning spell to the underglazes, so that an oily soup spoon or a messy spatula wouldn't leave the spoon rest covered in germs or even appearing dirty at all.

I gladly lost myself in the busyness of my role as clerk. It felt like a power of mine all its own how I could meet each person where they were, understand their need, and find just the right piece for them.

It was such a lovely morning that when Sasha came in to tell me I could go home, as my shift was over and hers was about to begin, I almost didn't want to leave.

But then I remembered my plans for that afternoon.

My stomach flip-flopped. If I'd thought that little snake had made me nervous...

The previous week, I'd accepted Ruby True's invitation to come over, without giving enough thought to what it would be like to spend time one-on-one with the older Fifth Wind. I won't lie, I found her incredibly intimidating. I'd only ever spent time with her when other people were around, and she seemed like one of those people who'd long since gotten over the idea that she should follow anyone else's rules. I had no idea what to expect from her, frankly.

She was also, I'd come to learn, one of the most magically powerful people in Eastwind, perhaps coming in behind only Liberty Freeman and the angelic powers of Sheriff Gabby Bloom.

When I'd accepted the invitation, "next week" had seemed far away. But now it was here, and I knew myself better than to think I would make up an excuse to skip the visit and risk having her hunt me down for a plausible explanation. Would she do it? Like I said, I really couldn't tell with her.

While Ruby left me slightly on edge, she didn't seem to register on Atlas's oversensitive danger-o-meter. Perhaps it was that he naturally trusted witches with hellhound familiars, but I suspected it was less psychologically complex than that. Grim had mentioned to us before that Ruby had always been generous with the bacon while he and Nora had boarded at her cottage. To make the visit even more enticing, Atlas enjoyed being around Ruby's familiar, Clifford. I couldn't blame him. Clifford was an old red-orange hellhound, who was a different kind of albino, apparently, but whose old bones made his favorite hobby lying by a warm fireplace all day. He almost never left the house, so I didn't know much about him, but Atlas had felt safe in his calm presence and had learned over the last winter to appreciate the comfort of a warm fire.

At the end of the day, though, it was probably the promise of bacon that prompted him to agree to come with me.

I'll be honest, I was glad he would be by my side when we visited Ruby's home. The place had a powerful aura to it that I'd found overwhelming the few times I'd stepped inside. And while Ruby's invitation to me had been friendly enough, she struck me as someone who could juggle multiple ulterior motives at once, satisfying them all without ever letting on.

Atlas met me at Fulcrum Park, which was roughly on my route. He was lying flat in what little snow was still on the ground, attempting to blend in as he hawkishly watched two young children chase each other around. Two men, presumably their fathers, chatted animatedly on a park bench, interrupting their own conversation to remind the children not to walk along the edge of the fountain.

"Good morning," I said, arriving next to my large white hellhound.

He popped up from the ground and shook snow off his fur. I could still see the faintest pink stain on his snout from all the beet pie he'd eaten two days before. *"Not a good morning. Monster was sticking her paw under the bedroom door all morning just to torment me. I was almost late."*

I patted him on the head, because what else was there to do but comfort him? I'd run out of ways to explain that the feral whims of the munchkin cat didn't have to rule his life, and that he could, in fact, adequately defend himself if she launched one of her sneak attacks. No matter how rational of an idea that was, though, it hadn't yet made it through the thick fog of his fear of her. In many ways, he was getting braver by the week, but he was still the same hellhound who had been bullied relentlessly in the Deadwoods for looking different from the pack. That sort of thing could take a long time to get over. I was willing to let him move at his own pace.

"Why are we going over to Ruby and Clifford's again?" he asked.

"Ruby invited us over. I mentioned to Nora that I didn't really know how to use the teapot that Dante gave me for the Winter Solstice. You know how people talk around town. Nora told Ruby, who is a big tea aficionado, apparently, and so Ruby invited me over for a tea lesson."

"Don't you have more important things to do?"

I smiled. "Not really. Isn't that lovely?" But then my mind wandered to all of the things I could've been busy with, like figuring out what was going on with the possibly dead animals at the studio or looking into who that mystery woman was sneaking around, or even spending time with Dante...

As we arrived on the doorstep of Ruby's blue attached cottage, I knocked (four times), and waited, clutching my woven bag at my side. My fingers ran up and down the shape of the teapot inside. He'd made this for me. Surely that meant *something*.

Or maybe it once did, but things have changed now that Izzy's back in town.

Ruby opened the door and greeted me with a smile. Even though it was well into the afternoon, she was wearing large orange slippers that resembled hellhound paws. "Come in, come in."

Atlas scented the air. *"Bacon!"*

"I have a little something for the cowardly lion," she said, ushering us by her. The reference from my old world was like cold water to my face. It was strange to hear something familiar from what felt like a lifetime ago. Nora had explained to me early on, though, that Ruby was also from our world. She'd been living up in the Midwest somewhere before she'd died and ended up in Eastwind. The idea that we shared a history with our old realm helped settle my nerves slightly as I paused just inside of the cottage door.

Clifford raised his head from his place by the fire, got a good glimpse of us, and *thumped* his tail on the rug a few times in greeting.

"Bacon?" I said.

"Of course. And because the smell of it lingers, I plan on us mixing up a tea with an aroma that will complement the scent rather than clash with it. You like rosemary, yes?"

I smiled politely. "Who doesn't?"

Ruby shuffled in her slippers toward the kitchen.

I took my time removing my coat and hanging it up by the door. It wasn't hard to understand why someone might describe Ruby's home as cozy. It had three floors to it, and the first floor contained the living room, which was hardly more than two wingback chairs by a warm fireplace, a small circular dining table in the center, and a small kitchen connected to the rest of the space. The only part of the bottom floor that wasn't open was the bathroom, which thankfully had a door that could shut. The floorboards appeared to be made of ancient wood, but that wasn't where my eyes went first when I entered this place. It was the ceiling that was the most interesting thing about her cottage. Strings of bells and bones, feathers and charms, and objects I couldn't quite name (and probably didn't care to) dangled from the ceiling in such a dense quantity that it made me want to duck my head as I stepped further inside, even though I had plenty of space above me.

Ruby True may have been a Fifth Wind witch like me, with a similar set of powers related to the spirit and death, but she'd been learning about her powers for much, much longer. She'd also learned witchcraft beyond the natural necromancy skills. One thing was clear: it was best not to assume that her age had made her any less powerful of a witch. I'd heard snippets of stories about her through the years, and each one was more unbelievable than the last. Yet I believed them all.

"Come and get it, boys," she said, jamming a spatula under each slab of bacon to pull it free of the cast-iron griddle.

Atlas was by her side in a heartbeat, but Clifford took

his time, grunting as he got to his feet and loping over somewhat stiffly.

Ruby was no taller than me, and so she had to extend
her arm to its full height to dangle a piece of bacon over
Atlas's head where he couldn't easily reach it without
jumping. "Sit," she said.

"*I'm not a pet dog,*" he griped. Then he sat.

"Good boy." She handed him the bacon.

After each of the familiars had been hand fed a few
strips, she divided the rest onto two plates, set those on the
floor by the fire for them to lick clean, and then washed up.

"Enough of that," she said, wiping her wet hands on her
layers of robes and shuffling over to the round table. "Show
me that teapot."

I took a seat across from her and set it on the table.

"Oooh..." She slid it closer, holding it up to get a look at
the bottom. Her full inspection included flipping the lid
around in her palm, pressing an eye right up against the
opening to look inside, and blowing air down the spout.
"That's a quality teapot," she concluded. "And a man gave
this to you?"

"Dante Fontaine, yes."

She grinned slyly. "Right, right. I've seen the two of you
out together." She whistled. "If I were forty years younger,
I'd fight you for that man."

I laughed. "And you'd probably win."

She winked at me. "I do know how to brew up a fierce
love potion. But don't worry, that's not what we're doing
today. Unless... you're interested?"

I won't deny considering it, as the image of Dante and
Izzy sitting together at Franco's Pizza flashed into my mind.
But ultimately, it didn't seem worth it. "No. With my luck,

it would go terribly wrong and he would end up in love with someone else."

Ruby narrowed her eyes at me. "If I helped you, it wouldn't go wrong." When I shook my head, she shrugged. "Have it your way. Tea it is. You can win a man's heart with a solid steep, anyhow."

I followed her into the kitchen where she lit a fire under the kettle and then pulled out a long wooden board along which no fewer than two dozen small boxes rested. She set the assortment on the countertop. "These are my ingredients."

I gazed over the boxes. They were ornate, with various colors of wood pattern on each. While none of them looked the same as any other, none of them were labeled. "You know what's in each of these?"

Ruby nodded. "I've been brewing tea a long time, dear. Normally, I just pull from one of those"—she pointed down the countertop to a row of three glass jars with tea mixes in them— "but I figure if we're going to have a lesson, we may as well start from the beginning."

I helped her pop off the lids, and the difference between the ingredients became quickly apparent by the aromas as well as the look of each. As she guided me through grabbing a pinch of this and a pinch of that, all of which we put into a smooth wooden bowl, she paused, her fingers hovering over one of the boxes. "I was thinking we could make bubble tea today."

"I've heard of that. Isn't it something with tapioca?"

"Hmm... not in Eastwind. Bubble tea is a specialty at A New Leaf. I got the recipe from the owner, and he connected me to his source for this particular ingredient."

I took a better look at the box her hand was hovering over. It looked like small bits of oyster mushrooms.

"Oh!" I said. "Oh. Yes, I remember hearing about that tea." I also remembered seeing Ruby and Ezra dance around the teashop euphorically after having drunk it.

Our eyes met.

"So?" she said. "It could be a good time."

I felt my heart race. "Are you sure it's okay?" I whispered.

Ruby threw her head back and laughed. "Whose permission do you need, dear?"

"I mean, is it legal?"

"What in the realm are you talking about? They sell it at A New Leaf. It's just a mushroom, Dahlia. Do you know what kind of magical tomfoolery happens around town every day that's far riskier? Just yesterday, I saw a leprechaun steal old Gladeth Lathly's broom and fly it into the side of Sheehan's Pub! You think anyone cares if we enjoy our tea? Bah! Besides, if it were for some strange reason outlawed, it's not like Gabby Bloom would come arrest me." She winked. "I have way too much dirt on the woman."

"What about Tanner?" I asked.

Ruby chuckled. "He could try. I have dirt on him, too, though. You know he once switched bodies with Grim? Not a pretty scene, especially when Grim forgot he was wearing Tanner's body and tried to lick his own—" She cut herself off. "Never mind that. The mushrooms simply elevate your mood, make you *feel* bubbly, hence the name. But we certainly don't have to if—"

"Okay, yes," I said, grabbing a pinch and throwing them in the wooden bowl. "I could use a little mood boost lately."

Ruby stared down at the bowl. "That might be more than a little. Why the hellhound not, though, huh? I have no plans for the next few hours."

Once we finished preparing our tea mix, we settled in back at the table, my teapot now containing the hot water from the kettle.

Ruby added the mixture to the pot, allowed it to steep for three minutes, then showed me how to properly pour into the cups. "Always serve others first," she instructed, "unless you hate them, then serve yourself and skip them entirely. That'll let them know where they stand with you." Once our cups were steaming hot with the bubble tea, she lifted hers and said, "Cheers."

"Cheers," I replied. The first sip was delicious. Too much so.

"So then I told Sebastian where he could stick those lying fangs of his," Ruby said, "and would you believe it, that pale face of his managed to drain of even more color!"

I roared with laughter and nearly fell out of my chair. Not because of the tea, though. It was genuinely a delightful and hilarious story.

When I slipped out of my chair and hit the ground, I had to admit that, okay, maybe it *was* the tea. At least slightly.

Not a single worry burdened my mind in that moment, though, and, wow, was that a nice feeling!

"Men," Ruby said, giggling but otherwise not seeming to notice that I had to lift myself off the ground. "They think we were born yesterday."

"I had no idea you and Sebastian ever dated."

"Oh, I wouldn't call it *that*."

We both giggled some more. "Well, you know what I mean. So when did you an Ezra start... whatever?"

"Whatever indeed!" She roared with laughter and finally calmed herself with another sip of the tea. "Years and years ago."

"Oh. But he doesn't look—"

"Don't let him fool you," she said, leaning over the table and wagging a finger at me. "He's as old as I am. A Peter Pan type. Never wanted to grow up, and in Eastwind, if you know the right people, you don't have to."

"Are you two together now?"

She shrugged. "Sometimes we find ourselves together, and sometimes we don't. He likes things casual."

"Ugh," I said. "I know the feeling."

"Men," she said.

"Men."

"To be fair," she added, "I like it casual, too." She cackled, and I tried not to spit out my sip of tea. "The closest thing to a serious relationship I've ever had since being here is my friendship with Gabby. The men come and go." She leaned forward conspiratorially and added, "I mostly like it when they go."

"*Can you keep it down over there?*" Clifford asked from the rug by the fireplace.

Ruby ignored him. "You want something serious with Dante, though, don't you?"

"Yes. Yes, I do," I said, allowing the clarity of the tea to awaken me to my own desires. "But I don't know that he wants it. In fact, I suspect he doesn't. There's this friend of his named Izzy who came back into town this week, and I think he might want to be with her instead."

Ruby leaned forward, locking eyes with me, her expression suddenly serious. "Want me to curse her?" We both howled with laughter. My stomach was starting to hurt from the unseriousness of our conversation, but I never wanted it to stop.

"Maybe just a little curse," I said. "Give her some boils or something." Who was that speaking? Surely those words hadn't just come out of *my* mouth. But no denying it, they had.

"Cheers to that!" She emptied out the last of the tea into our cups then said, "How about some music? I feel like dancing!"

I felt like dancing, too, come to think of it.

As Ruby pulled a wand out of her robes and flicked it into the air, lively music filled the room.

"Hey," I said, having to raise my voice to be heard. "Have you ever brought anything back to life by accident?"

She was already on her feet and boogying as she replied, "Used to do it all the time! Part of learning your powers! Once raised a sizeable army of the dead. Wouldn't recommend that. If it happens, though, just make sure you don't get caught!"

Seemed like sound enough advice for the time being, so I stood up and joined her in dancing to the music as Clifford snored by the fire and Atlas kept a close eye on me, no doubt making sure I didn't try anything reckless that he would need to distance himself from.

As the tea's potency started to fade away, and Ruby plated two croissants for us to nosh on, I was still feeling quite good. The things that had burdened my heart felt much more distant, but they began to reoccupy my mind as I stared down at the now-empty teapot. "I wish I could make something nice like this for him."

"For whom, dear?"

"Dante. I'm not good enough at pottery yet to make anything nearly this lovely. At best, I could make him a mug with a crooked handle."

Ruby waved me off. "He didn't make this for you because he wanted a gift in return. My guess is that he made it for you because you were already gifting him something. Perhaps something you aren't aware of."

I shrugged. "If that were the case, why would he want to keep things casual?"

"Did he say that?"

"Yeah, he—" I paused.

"Ah, you read into his words. Best not to do that when it comes to men. You'll be much happier if you take everything they say at face value, trust me. And even if he does want to keep it casual, don't take it personally. It's never about you, dear. It's always about them." She gnawed off a big bite of croissant and spoke around it, "That being said, if you want commitment, then you want commitment. In all my years, the only way I ever stood a chance of receiving what I want from a man was to ask for it directly. Maybe he'll give it, and I'll be grateful for that. But maybe he won't, and I'll be grateful for that, too."

"Grateful he said to you what you wanted?" I asked.

"Grateful I know it's time to find a new man."

"Then I take it you never asked Ezra for commitment?"

She paused, sighed deeply, and seemed to become lost in a reverie. "I did once. He refused. So, I moved on."

"But I thought the two of you were together now."

"Bah," she said, waving me off playfully. "Not in the way you're thinking. We're probably in love, sure. I'm the only woman he's ever deeply wanted with his body, mind, and soul, yes. And we enjoy each other's company, which might be the most important piece. But until he knocks it off with his fear of aging, I'm not waiting up for him. I'm growing old at a beautifully natural pace and enjoying every second of it, despite what my joints have to say from time to time."

I couldn't help but stare at her like she was the eighth wonder. Ruby knew exactly who she was and what she wanted. Could I ever be like that? Would it take me another forty years?

"Dante's a good boy," she said. "Be bold, I say. If you know what you want, ask for it."

"That's my problem," I replied, "I don't *really* know what I want. Sometimes I think I do, but it never seems like it's worth the effort to go after it."

She narrowed her eyes at me. "I'm sure that's not correct. Maybe rather than asking what you want, you ought to start asking why you're scared to want anything at all."

"Ouch," I said, pulling off a hunk of the croissant. "You're not pulling any punches, are you?"

Ruby laughed. "Desire is painful! Experience it anyway!" Her gaze traveled to an old cuckoo clock on the wall. "My! Time has flown by. Nearly three hours in the blink of an eye. The tea will do that." She pushed herself out of her chair. "I've had a lovely time with you, Dahlia, but now I need you gone. I told Ezra he's taking me out to dinner tonight. I need to get ready. It takes a little longer nowadays than it used to."

I hurried to my feet and grabbed the teapot, sliding it back into my bag. "Thanks for the tea. And the pep talk. You know, I think I'd like for Dante to take me out tonight, too!"

Ruby approached me and placed a warm hand on my back. At first, I thought she was being motherly, then I realized she was steering me toward the door. "Good, good. Tell him that. If he's got any brains at all, he'll agree *and* make the plans."

"*Come on, Atlas,*" I called over my shoulder as Ruby shoved my coat at me.

Before she shut the door behind us, she added, "Be good and have fun!"

"You, too," I replied.

"I'll do one but not the other. You can guess which." The door shut behind me, and I had a very good idea which of those two options she would worry about, and which would get no further thought from the wild witch.

CHAPTER EIGHT

Atlas and I made our way back to Nora and Tanner's house to regroup. I wasn't feeling tired after the day of work and the visit to Ruby's house, but I did feel like I had a lot to think about, and my favorite place to do that was always in bed.

Before I settled in, though, I grabbed a parchment slip from the stationery box just inside Nora and Tanner's door and wrote Dante a note. It said, *Any interest in taking me to dinner tonight?*

I imagined Ruby would've phrased it differently to Ezra, maybe more like, *Where are you taking me for dinner tonight?* or even *You're taking me to dinner. Pick me up at 6.*

That was only aspirational for me, though. Even asking him if he had any interest felt like a big step. I was opening myself up for rejection, wasn't I?

I hesitated after writing the note. What if he said no? What if he didn't respond at all? Ouch.

Then I remembered what Ruby had told me. What he does or says isn't about me. It's about him. I wasn't sure I one hundred percent agreed with that, but I pretended I did all the same.

I offered the message to the spotted owl, who appeared when I rang the little brass bell. The owl received the parchment impassively in its talons and then took off in the direction of Dante. The owls somehow had a system for knowing the name of everyone in town and where each person was at any given moment, and as I watched it fly away, I guessed from its direction that it was going to Franco's Pizza, where Dante must still be finishing his day shift.

Surprisingly, I fell asleep almost instantly once I laid down in bed to think. Perhaps Atlas's warm body against my legs played a part, but I also didn't have the usual thoughts racing through my head that normally helped me stay awake (and I use the word "help" loosely, because I often didn't appreciate the assistance). I likely had the tea to thank. All I felt when my head hit the pillow was contentment, a rightness to the world, and a total lack of concern about what may happen in any moment outside of the present. My usual anxieties felt like none of my business.

The mail bell rang just over an hour later.

Groggy, with heavy limbs and a slight stinging behind my eyes, I dragged myself to the mailbox where the owl had dropped Dante's reply. I blinked blurriness away from my eyes as I unrolled the piece of parchment and began to read.

> *Just read your message (I was finishing up side-work and didn't realize a message had come for me). I already have plans with Izzy for dinner, but you're of course welcome to join. We're going to Stews and*

Brews for steaks. Meet at 8. Let me know if we need to change the reservation to three people.
    -Dante

Whatever contentment and peace I'd felt before falling asleep vanished like someone waved a wand at it.

Dinner plans with Izzy two nights in a row? Ruby's words to me about taking Dante at face value suddenly felt hollow and false. It was clear he was being nice and inviting me, but if he'd really wanted me there, he would've included me sooner. He wouldn't have waited until I reached out for him to tack me onto the reservation.

Dante was nothing if not nice. Maybe too nice. He probably didn't have the heart to tell me that he liked Izzy more.

Atlas peeked his head into the entryway, doing a quick scan to make sure Monster wasn't hiding, ready to pounce. *"Everything okay? No emergencies?"*

Everything was definitely not okay, so I said, "No emergencies. You hungry?"

"He said yes to dinner?"

"Not with me. Let's grab takeout somewhere."

He wagged his tail at the suggestion, as I began to hatch a plan, one that might take my mind off the soul-crushing pain I was feeling from reading Dante's reply. "How would you feel about joining me for a stakeout?"

Atlas's hackles rose. *"That sounds dangerous."*

I should've figured. "I'll buy you meatloaf if you come with me."

His ears perked up. *"I'm suddenly feeling much braver."*

CHAPTER NINE

I stopped by Helga's Savory Pies for dinner because it had the best chicken pot pie I'd ever had in my life, and I was in a mood where a warm, filling dinner sounded like heaven.

I entered the small bakery, which only had the space for four two-top tables, all of which were currently occupied. The rich smell of fresh-from-the-oven pastries reinforced that I'd made the right decision. I hadn't been by there in nearly a month, due mostly to my tight budget. But what was money for if not to make sure you had comfort food when you needed it? Ted had once confirmed for me that we couldn't take money with us when we died, so I might as well use it to numb my uncomfortable feelings with creamy chicken and a flaky crust. If a few vegetables made an appearance, I supposed I'd let it slide.

I was so busy staring lustily at the offerings behind the glass display case that I was shocked when I made it to the front of the line and saw who was working the counter.

"Wayne!" I said.

The leprechaun's face lit up. "You remember me?"

"Of course I do." Wayne had previously been a servant at Muscoff Manor Inn, back before the innkeeper was arrested. Long story. He'd done most of the work around the place, and I'd hoped that he might one day quit that awful job that had him working around the clock for almost no paycheck at all.

"I owe you so much, Miss Wildes. We all do. Gloriana was a bad, bad woman."

"I don't know about that," I said quietly, hoping none of the patrons were staring at me. "You don't work at the inn anymore, then?"

"Absolutely not, miss. No. The second you gave me that feather, it was like a storm cleared in my head. I ran out of that place and never looked back. I was so glad when I heard you'd survived. I couldn't have stayed to rescue you, you understand that, don't you?" He was staring at me with a pained expression that I was eager to relieve him of.

"Of course I understand that, Wayne. Of course. I'm glad you got out when you could. Are they better to you here?"

His face lit up. "A hundred times better, Miss Wildes! A thousand times! They pay me every Friday, not just when they feel like it. And they pay me enough that I can rent an apartment all my own!"

"Sounds wonderful," I replied, my attention drifting back to my pot pie plans.

"All but one thing, miss. No, I probably shouldn't say it."

Oh, now I was curious. "You can tell me. What is it?"

He looked around, didn't appear to see whomever he needed to avoid overhearing him, and murmured, "They don't let me work enough. There are entire shifts that someone else covers. What am I supposed to do if I'm not working?"

"I suppose you could try out a new hobby."

He squinted at me like I might be suffering a neurological catastrophe.

"Never mind," I said. "Maybe you could get a second job?"

"A second job! Great idea, miss. You keep helping me, over and over again! How can I ever repay the favor?"

I really didn't mean to be rude, but it'd been a rough day, and I was quite hungry. "Take my order?"

Wayne had done his best to insist that he pay for our entire order, but against the best interests of my personal finances, I talked him out of it. He didn't owe me a thing, after all.

True to my promise, I ordered Atlas a whole meatloaf all to himself. Oh, and I might've splurged on a bottle of red wine for myself.

I wasn't sad to leave the adoring but watchful gaze of Wayne as we left the bakery. It was a little too much, and all I wanted was to get going on the stakeout so I could be alone with my carbs and booze.

We made our way to the studio quickly, before our dinners could get cold.

"If that woman I told you about comes back, I'll be able to catch her," I explained as we brought our dinner into the Time to Kiln studio through the back door.

"And then what? You'll fight her?"

"I don't think it will come to that. I just want to know who she is and why she's leaving dead animals in the studio."

"Something sinister, I'm sure."

"Maybe, or maybe not," I said. *"We don't know yet."*

Was this stakeout a distraction from thinking about Dante and Izzy's no-doubt intimate dinner plans? Probably. Should I have responded to his message instead of saying nothing? Also probably.

To be fair, I was genuinely curious about what was going on at the studio as well. My chat with Ruby had confirmed that, yes, I was probably resurrecting the dead animals without meaning to. She didn't have to tell me twice to keep that fact to myself. I required a little space to process the implications of how I'd been playing God, albeit unintentionally.

Knowing the critters had all been dead when I'd found them didn't answer the other questions I still had, like who was that woman I'd seen sneaking around the back of the studio? Was she the one leaving those dead animals for me? And if so, why would anyone do that? Was it a threat?

I was pretty sure Raven and Jude wouldn't be mad at me for staying in the studio overnight. After all, they'd given Grace a key to it back when Monty was sleeping poorly due to a growth spurt, and she wasn't even an employee. Even more, they'd invited her to come by and throw on the wheel at odd hours of the night, whenever Landon took over. Grace was the kind of person who needed a hefty amount of silence each day, and I could only imagine how much the non-stop crying of a small child got to her after weeks of it. Raven and Jude must've seen it in her face.

I pulled out a small table and chair from the break area so that I had a clear view of the back door of the studio, and then I set out my pot pie, grabbed one of the community mugs from a hook, popped the wine cork, and poured myself a mugful of red.

I portioned out the meatloaf to Atlas, only serving him a quarter of it at a time and adding breaks between servings; he had no self-control when a plate of meat was in front of him, and I'd been learning the hard way that if I let him at it without slowing down the process, I'd be smelling the consequences of it all night.

Once settled in, I started to wonder: who else might have a key to the studio?

Jude and Raven, of course—they owned the place— then there was me and Sasha, since we worked there and we switched off opening shifts every so often. Grace had a key. Did Dante have one? Any other students?

Could the woman with the hair and jacket that looked like mine have a key?

That probably depended on who the heck she was.

What would Nora do? I asked.

Well, first of all, she would probably be too busy running Medium Rare and investigating murders to worry about this little mystery.

Then again, there *were* murders. Murders of two mice and a snake. Those lives still mattered to me. Maybe there were no ghosts around for me to interview, but every creature—big and small—deserved protection and someone who cared about what happened to them.

I checked the clock on the wall. It was already past 9 pm. After my shift the following day, I could go to the store where I bought my coat and see if they knew who else had bought one. Yes, that's what a real detective would do. If I were going to pretend to be one, I might as well go all out.

The stakeout was serving its purpose of distracting

me quite nicely, and once I worked my way through the delicious pot pie and the entire bottle of wine—whoops!—there was not much thinking left to do, only waiting and fighting against how heavy my eyelids had become.

I woke up with a start, not quite sure of where I was, but vaguely aware of something soft against my cheek.

I rubbed my eyes. I was in the studio. The lights were mostly off except for one right over the back door. And I was on the ground. But it was soft?

Pulling my head off of Atlas's side, which I'd been using as a pillow, I vaguely remembered grabbing a few cushions from the sofa in the break room and creating a makeshift bed on the hard studio floor.

My head swam as I rubbed my cheek, finding a texture on it from indentations of my familiar's fur.

I'd been sleeping, but something woke me up. It was a noise. A repetitive noise.

My brain snapped online, and I realized it was a chirping. Well, half chirping, half squawking.

I dragged a hand down my face, trying to make sense of everything through the start of a wine hangover, and then crawled to my feet and hit a light switch.

A little sparrow flitted awkwardly from the edge of a greenware shelf to the floor. It tried to hop into the air again, but failed, and landed in the same place, chirping loudly.

"*Don't move,*" said Atlas, "*and it might not attack.*"

I hadn't noticed that he was fully awake with his eyes

locked on the bird. He'd been so still while I used him as a pillow that I'd assumed he was asleep.

"It won't attack us," I whispered. "How'd it get in here?"

"No idea. A hellhound's gotta sleep, too, ya know."

"So, it snuck in while we were sleeping?" I said. No, that didn't sound right. Birds didn't sneak.

I approached it slowly, crooning, "You're okay. Just stay there."

Once I was close enough, I saw what all the fuss was about. One of its wings was bent at an unnatural angle. "Ouchy," I said. "I'm sorry you're hurt. Can I help you?"

While I didn't get a sense that this bird was anyone's familiar, it stopped its squawking and flailing, and turned to look at me directly, tilting its head.

"How did you get in here?" I asked, then, realizing that was a silly question to ask unless one of my magical powers was speaking sparrow, I said, "Can I help you?" and held out my hands to it. It didn't try to fly off, and instead took a small hop closer to me. I knelt down and set my open palms faceup on the floor. "Come on. It looks like you've hurt your wing. I have a friend who helps animals feel better. I can bring you there if you'll let me."

The bird blinked, then took another hop closer. I let my eyes travel to the clock on the wall. It wasn't yet 7am. I could make it to Zoe Clementine's animal sanctuary and back before I had to open the shop, if I didn't dilly dally too much.

Besides, the cold morning air would probably help with this blossoming hangover that pounded against the inside of my skull.

The bird moved closer, but didn't go all the way into

my hands. So I moved my hands closer to it, and when it didn't run away, I went for it and scooped it up. It didn't struggle, which I was glad about, since I didn't want the wing to sustain any more injury than it already had.

"Want to come to Zoe's with me?" I asked Atlas.

"*No, that place gives me the creeps. I'll wait for you here.*" But he did follow me out the door to take care of his morning business.

It had snowed again overnight, so as he kicked up a white cloud with his back paws, I made my way in the morning darkness to the other side of town to get the little bird some help.

The cold air did wonders for my headache, and I was able to think more clearly. The first thought that came crashing in was clear enough: this bird was lucky to be alive. No doubt it had almost fallen victim to the same thing as the two mice and that little snake.

But more chillingly, that means someone had been in the studio while I slept and left the sparrow for me. Someone had crept in, seen me sleeping there, and snuck out—all without either Atlas or me knowing. I didn't like how vulnerable that had made me. Not at all.

Who had that access? Who was that stealthy? And why were they leaving dead and injured animals for me to find?

CHAPTER TEN

By the time I returned from the animal sanctuary, feeling certain that the little sparrow was in the best of hands with Zoe Clementine, my wine headache was mostly gone. I still felt a little groggy and sluggish, but that could've been from sleeping poorly more than from the alcohol.

The post-Blue Sky Festival shoppers coming into Time to Kiln had begun to wane, so I didn't have all that much to do once I opened the shop. A few folks came in to browse, but no one seemed in the buying mood. I regretted deeply not stopping somewhere on my way back from the sanctuary to get breakfast and a coffee.

Atlas snoozing at my feet, I sat at my desk calculating the minutes left until the end of my shift, after which I could go ask around about who else had bought a coat identical to mine. The bell above the front door rang, and Dante stepped inside. His gaze locked onto me, and he didn't look happy *at all*.

"There you are," he said. I was blasted by a wave of

emotions that weren't mine—a mixture of hurt, anger, and self-righteousness. Yikes! I slumped down in my seat.

Had neglecting to respond to his message really set him off like this? I'd only ever seen him show this much aggression once before, and it was right before he fought Brunt Scandrick outside of Sheehan's Pub. And even then, the aggression hadn't been aimed at me but rather on my behalf. There was no mistaking it now, though: Dante was angry with *me*.

I appreciated the physical barrier of the desk that kept him a few feet away from me when he planted his feet. But even with the desk there, his emotions were so thick in the air that they practically choked me. "What's your problem, huh?" he demanded.

I shook my head vaguely, mouth gaping. Atlas jumped to his feet, his hackles raised as he stood next to the desk and bared his teeth at Dante.

"Don't act like you have no idea what I'm talking about," he said. "I know you've been hiding from me since you stormed out. Were you really not home last night, or did you make Nora lie for you when I showed up?"

"I—I really wasn't home. I'm sorry, Dante, I should've responded to your message. I just—"

He held up a hand to stop me. The corners of his mouth turned down in an expression of disgust. "Please, you know that's not what it's about. I'll take a lot from someone I care about, but I do have *some* lines I won't let anyone cross. Not even you."

I tried to land on a single clarifying question I could ask, but I didn't know where to start.

"If you didn't want me going to dinner with a *friend* of mine, why didn't you just say something? If you'd said a single word about it—*I don't want you spending time with her, Dante*—anything, I would've changed my plans. Instead, you said nothing, showed up at the restaurant, and made a scene by yelling at me?"

My jaw dropped even further. I could technically make out the words coming from his mouth, but none of them were fully penetrating my complete confusion. "What?"

His upper lip curled. "Please. Just drop the act. It's not like you to play dumb. Then again, I also thought it wasn't like you to cause a scene and hit me rather than just talking about what's bothering you like an adult. So maybe I'm learning all kinds of things about you, Dahlia."

"I'm so sorry," I said meekly. "I don't... I don't understand."

"Where did you sleep last night, huh? If you weren't home, where were you? You trying to get back at me? Make me jealous by staying with some other guy?"

The suggestion that I might try something that petty shocked me. I didn't mean to laugh as I said, "What?" but I was so out of my element here. What the hellhound was he even talking about?

"I'm right then, huh? You didn't expect me to guess. You said you'd do as much last night, anyway." He took a step back toward the door. "You know what? Fine. Nothing was ever going on with me and Izzy, but I'm glad you thought it was, because this has really showed me who you are."

He turned and walked out, the ringing of the bell above the door sounding more like a death knell.

Atlas slowly lowered his hackles once it was obvious that the threat had left and wasn't returning. *"That was scary."*

"*Scary, confusing, and a bunch of other things,*" I replied, my mind swirling like a dust storm. Atlas was visibly shaking after his instinctual act of bravery. It wouldn't be until my own adrenaline had crashed that I could fully appreciate him for it.

"Did I leave the studio at some point last night?" I asked.

It felt like a slim chance, but I *did* down a bottle of wine and forgot most of the evening after that.

Atlas shook his fluffy white head. "*If you did, I never saw it. I think I would've heard you come and go.*"

"You didn't hear whoever brought the sparrow inside coming and going."

"*No, but you were at no risk of being stealthy after all that wine.*"

"Then what in the realm happened in that restaurant with Dante?"

"*I don't know,*" said Atlas, "*but I have a bad feeling about it.*"

I reached down and scratched his head. Only then did I realize that I was shaking just as much as he was. "I do, too, boy. Something strange is going on in town. I can't pin it down yet, but I know I don't like it one bit."

I felt starkly alone as the rest of the day unfolded. It was as if a ghost of me was the one speaking with customers, while the rest of me was off somewhere on a desert island. Atlas kept checking in with me, but even my connection with him felt oddly distant.

Dante's ire had scared me, even though I hadn't felt at

any point that he was on the verge of physical violence. His toxic cocktail of emotions still clung to my skin.

He believed I'd chewed him out. In public. But I couldn't have. I was asleep on old sofa cushions, using my familiar as a pillow, not out seeking retribution for him spending time with Izzy.

Confusing particulars aside, Dante now believed I was a terrible person. He'd sounded completely done with me. Would he ever speak to me again? I tried to comprehend the complete change of circumstances from the boldness I'd felt about our relationship leaving Ruby's cottage the day before to the way I wanted to shrink into something smaller than an atom after the way he'd yelled at me.

And the strangest thing was, I didn't feel like he was lying. I didn't have an internal lie detector like Sheriff Bloom, but there was something about his conviction, about his indignation that told me he genuinely believed what he was saying. How that made any sense at all was unknown to me.

"You okay?"

The familiar voice pulled me out of my fog, and I looked around the shop until I saw Grace popping her head out of the studio. Was it already that late in the day? She usually didn't come until later in the afternoon during the week to work on her pottery projects.

"Huh? Oh, yeah, I'm fine."

She took a step further into the shop, her eyed narrowed. "You didn't look fine. You didn't look like you were in this realm."

I forced a smile. "Long day."

"Wanna talk about it?"

I weaved my fingers into the fur on Atlas's head.

"Nothing to talk about. I just skipped lunch. Guess I'm a little spacy. Sasha should be in soon to take over."

She nodded slowly, though it was clear she was unconvinced. "If you change your mind, let me know. I'm always here to talk."

I wished I could've said yes. I wished I could've told her not only what had happened with Dante, but how it'd left me feeling. Running through a solid brick wall would've been an easier feat in that moment, though. For one, Grace and Dante were good friends. What if she took his side? She was a logical person, and so was Dante. I was the emotional one. I was the illogical one. Whatever he said about the events would probably make more sense. He wasn't one to lie, either. Clearly, *someone* had shouted at him.

Yet there was something else stopping me from opening up to my best friend. Something I was quite familiar with from my life in New Orleans: loneliness. The profoundness of being alone, but also the sense that I deserved to stay that way.

Dante's anger had returned me to that small life I used to live, where I was utterly alone. Perhaps reaching out was the antidote to loneliness, maybe saying, "I feel lonely" was exactly what a person ought to do to combat the emotion, but as anyone who's been there knows, loneliness has a way of keeping you trapped in it, convincing you that it's inevitable, perhaps even your destiny.

So I maintained the forced smile until Grace relented and disappeared into the studio again.

Atlas lumbered to his feet from his spot on the floor. *"Okay then,"* he said, *"we'd better figure out what the hellhound is going on. I don't want to fight Dante, but I will."*

I felt a crack form along the edge of my loneliness. A deep warmth spread through my chest. I leaned over, hugged Atlas around his thick neck, and cried as silently as I could into his fur.

This wasn't New Orleans. This was Eastwind. And thanks to him, I'd never be truly alone again.

CHAPTER ELEVEN

My plan was to go to Hagseed Café to grab some dinner, because I had skipped lunch, and because it was on the opposite side of town from Franco's Pizza and Dante's home. It was also not nearly fancy enough for a date night, so I was sure I wouldn't run into him and Izzy there. (My stomach churned to even consider it.)

I left through the front of the shop to avoid the possibility of another conversation with Grace, who was busy at the wheel trying to perfect a moon jar. The cold nipped at my ears, and I popped the collar of my coat and stuck my hands deep into my pockets. Had it really been only last weekend that we enjoyed blue skies overhead? How much in my life here had changed since then? Since yesterday, really?

Atlas stayed glued to my left side, which was great news for that side, as it remained much toastier than the rest of me. The streets were busy with the evening bustle, and I was grateful to be lost in the crowd. Or at least as lost in a crowd as one could be when there was a massive albino hellhound at your side.

I could feel the anxiety flowing off him—he hated crowds due to "the extreme risk of being ambushed with bops to the head"—but I was likely the only one who could sense his current level of fear. He'd puffed himself up big and was making an admirable effort to keep his tail from tucking between his legs. I knew why he was doing it, and I loved him even more deeply for it. No doubt his adrenaline would crash as soon as we made it back to Nora and Tanner's house, and he would sleep like a log through the night. Probably snore, too. That was fine with me. His loyalty was more than earning any possible future snores.

I began to wonder, as we passed by familiar faces and I nodded and smiled at a few that I knew well, if the word had gotten out about me confronting Dante. What would people think of me when they found out? Would all the work Nora and Ruby had done to earn Fifth Winds a better reputation be laid to waste by what I'd done?

Now, don't you start believing it, my inner voice lectured me. *You didn't do anything. Someone did, but it wasn't you.*

Right. But it didn't matter what I knew, if others at the restaurant with Dante and Izzy had seen someone who looked like me there, shouting at him and generally acting unhinged. Rumors were rumors, and I'd already seen how quickly word got around here.

I picked up the pace to Hagseed Café, ordered quickly, and took the food—a decadent grilled cheese and creamy tomato soup—to-go.

Don't worry, I ordered Atlas everything he wanted from the menu, even though it left my pockets nearly empty of coins. I would likely have to go a little hungry until my pay day later that week, but I didn't mind. He deserved it. He deserved the world.

To avoid the busyness of Fulcrum Park at the center of town, I took a longer route to the house, and found myself walking along dark cobblestone streets with so little foot traffic that I could hear the last bits of crunchy snow beneath my boots with every slow step I took.

But I also heard something else, now that I was away from the bustle. There was the crunch beneath Atlas's paws, but there was something more. Someone more. Another set of steps off rhythm with ours.

Outside of a few intense near-death encounters on investigations, I'd never felt unsafe in Eastwind. It hadn't occurred to me to avoid walking around in the dark. But something inside of me shouted that I needed to check over my shoulder, so I did.

My jaw nearly hit the ground when I saw who was walking only ten yards behind me.

With hair identical to mine and a coat exactly like the one I currently had pulled tightly around me, it was... me.

"You." I said. Then I corrected myself. "Me."

Atlas's hackles were raised high as we stared at the woman who'd been following quietly behind us.

"*I don't like this at all,*" he said, his telepathic voice shaky. Poor guy was probably tapped from having to play it tough for most of our route.

The woman—me—smiled at us as she continued sauntering forward, closing the space. "Don't tell me you're afraid of yourself," she said, before addressing Atlas with, "Don't you recognize me? I'm your witch."

"If you're my witch, then I'm the backside of a unicorn," he replied. She didn't react.

Of course she didn't. She couldn't hear him. Only I could. She wasn't me. Couldn't be.

She paused within a few feet of us. It was like looking in a mirror. Except there was something internal about her that was different. Something missing. Or maybe she had something I didn't. I tried to tune in and use my Empathy to get a read on what she was feeling. Maybe it would help me make sense of what was going on. But try as I might, I couldn't sense any emotions from her. It was like trying to read the words from a blank page.

"Surprised to see me?" she said.

"Surprised doesn't even touch it," I replied. "Who are you?"

She shrugged playfully. "I'm you."

"Nooo," I said. "You're not. I'm me. But you're..." It clicked. "You accosted Dante at dinner last night!"

She grinned and held up her hands. "Guilty. Are you going to tell me I shouldn't have?"

"Of course! You can't go around making scenes like that!"

"Says who? It's what you wanted to do, isn't it?"

"That's beside the point! I mean... no. It's *not* what I wanted to do. I would never do that." The fact that I was raising my voice at myself like this was confusing, and I dialed it back as best I could. "But he thinks I did it."

"You did."

"I didn't! You did, and you know it. Yet I'm the one who got yelled at for it, and now he'll never speak to me again."

"Why, because I told him the truth?"

"The truth about what?" I said.

"The truth about his childish behavior. After all this time we've spent together since I came to Eastwind, I shouldn't have to play the understanding and endlessly patient side chick while he goes out to dinner, night after night, with some pretty girl from his past. I shouldn't have to feel like an afterthought in his plans. I deserve better treatment than that!"

I felt my blood start to boil. This day had been too much for me. "What are you talking about?" I demanded. "*You* weren't the one he kissed at the Winter Solstice party. *You* weren't the one he made that teapot for. And *you* weren't the one getting left out of his plans all week while he hung out with Izzy! I was!"

"You're right," she said simply. "It was you. So why was I the one who had the guts to show up at the restaurant last night and stand up for us?"

I was too angry with her to let her win. "I don't even know who you are! Or *what* you are! Or... *how* you are! But listen here, you've screwed up everything I had going with Dante—"

"I'd say he screwed it up and you didn't fight for it—"

I held up a hand to silence her. "*You* screwed it up. Period, end of story. So now you need to come with me to find him and explain this whole thing. If he sees both of us together, he'll understand how it's possible that it wasn't me yelling at him last night."

She seemed to consider it, tapping a finger to her chin. "Hmm... No. I don't think I will." She turned and started walking away from us, a swagger in each step.

I tried a different tack: "Please?" I called.

"Nope."

I felt myself panicking. "What am I supposed to do?"

She paused, a dozen yards away now, and looked back over her shoulder. "Forget what you're supposed to do. Why not do what you *want* to do for once? I've gotten us started already. Keep up the streak."

I watched her disappear, trying to think of a comeback, some retort that would convince her to reconsider. My brain didn't work that quickly, though, especially when I was this flustered.

Do whatever I want to do? If I'd done what I wanted to do right then, I would've chased after her, tackled her to the ground, and made Atlas drag her around town with us until we found Dante. That was impossible, though. I'd never actually do that.

Just before she disappeared from view, she hollered, "It's a nice coat. You have good taste."

Atlas and I stood staring in the silence of the side street.

"*Nope, didn't like that at all,*" he finally said.

"Thanks for not running away."

"*I would've, but I was frozen in place.*"

I scratched him behind the ears. "Let's get going. I think it's well past time to have a chat with Nora about... whatever the heck is going on."

It was never a dull day in Eastwind, that was for sure.

CHAPTER TWELVE

Nora wasn't home when we arrived, so I set out my soup and sandwich on the dining room table and was determined to wait for her in that spot. Once Atlas had his dinner laid out in my bedroom so Monster and Grim couldn't get at it, he could fall right to sleep on the bed afterward. I settled in and did the best I could at enjoying my grilled cheese and tomato soup. They weren't hot anymore, but they were warm enough, and the bread had the perfect balance of toastiness to grease to turn the volume down on my swimming thoughts.

The front door opened as I was spooning out the last of my soup. I heard the familiar sound of her keys being tossed into a small knickknack bowl I'd made at the studio, heard her shaking the snow off the bottom of her coat before hanging it on the rack, and a loud declaration of, "Fang's sake, it's still too cold out there!"

She appeared in the kitchen and spotted me. "Whatever that is, it smells good."

"Oh, sorry," I said. "I should've grabbed something for you, too." Not like I had the money, but still.

She waved me off. "No need to say sorry. I just came from a diner, you know. A diner I own. I'm all set on food when I need it." She went to the icebox, opened it, and pulled out a glass bottle. "This is the only thing I need right now." She popped the top of the beer and took a long sip. "Lot Flufferbum's decided to compile a list of the best restaurants in Eastwind for the *Eastwind Watch*. I'm sure he has big aspirations of selling it to some travel magazine in Avalon, too. He's been dangling the list over every restaurant owner's head this week, and today he decided it was our turn for a visit at Medium Rare. Ordering everything on the menu like some wealthy prince, expecting all of our servers to make him a priority over the other guests. I'll be honest, Dahl, I don't even care about making that werebunny's dumb list. We're an Outskirts diner, and we like it that way. The *last* thing we need is a bunch of Avalonian tourists coming around, complaining that the experience isn't what they were hoping for. Because of course it won't be. It's not for them. It's for the regulars who just want a cheap burger and fries at the end of a long day." She paused to take another swig from her beer. "I just don't want to give Flufferbum the opportunity to stick us on some 'failing establishments' list he makes up, which he not-so-subtly implied he was also working on."

"Would that hurt business?" I asked.

Nora gave it some thought, squinting one eye. "Nah, probably not, come to think of it. I mean, heck, there was a murder at Medium Rare my first day in town, and nobody stopped going." She nodded at me. "Good call. Who cares what Flufferbum thinks? Jerk." She walked over to the table and took a seat across from me. "How was your day?"

My default pushed me toward saying "fine," but that was so not the case. I sighed. "I had a bad day. And a weird day."

She arched an eyebrow at me. "Do tell. Oh wait! Does this have anything to do with Dante coming by last night looking for you? He seemed upset. He also didn't seem like he believed me when I said you weren't home."

"Yeah, it has something to do with that. But I don't really understand what. Or how. I'm just... confused."

"Dating men will do that."

If I wasn't crashing so hard from the day, I would've laughed.

I started my story with Dante's blow-up on me, which forced me to fill her in on the backstory with Izzy, which I hadn't mentioned to anyone yet. Nora listened intently, and I could see theories already forming behind her eyes.

"And who is this Izzy chick?" she said.

"An old friend, according to Dante."

She nodded tentatively. "I can ask Jane about it, if you want. But go on. He yelled at you for... what exactly?"

"For crashing his dinner, yelling at him, and smacking him."

Nora chuckled and leaned back in her chair. "I didn't know you had it in you."

"I don't," I said. "It wasn't me."

"But he thought it was."

"Exactly."

Nora's expression turned serious. "And you're *sure* you didn't, like, black out at any point last night?"

"Well, I had a bottle of wine," I conceded, "but I'm pretty sure I just fell asleep on Atlas."

"Hold on, fell asleep on Atlas *where?*"

"At the studio. I was doing a stakeout. It's... it's a long story."

"We have time to get the facts straight."

I filled her in on the dead mice and snake and the bird with the broken wing.

"That *is* strange," she said quietly. "Also, welcome to accidental necromancy."

"Ruby already told me it happened sometimes."

Nora nodded. "Still strange about the dead and injured animals. That's usually not *nothing*, but perhaps it's unrelated to the stuff with Dante and Izzy?"

"I thought so too, but then I saw someone trying to get into the studio."

"Did you recognize them?"

"Uh... Well, yes, I did."

She leaned forward, waiting for me to go on. "And who was it?"

I took a deep breath. I'd never felt less sane telling a story. "In retrospect, I think it was me."

Nora closed her eyes and shook her head. "Come again?"

"It looked like me. And then on my way home tonight, I saw her again. And she... yes, it was me. She was even wearing the same clothes."

"Fangs and claws," Nora said, smacking her hand to her forehead. "Oh, fangs and claws. Please not this again."

"Not what?"

"Did you speak with her?"

"I did. She's the one who confronted Dante in the restaurant. She admitted to it."

Nora looked positively morose. "At least if someone else did go to the restaurant, we can rule out the possibility that you were possessed and simply didn't remember doing it yourself."

"That... nice to know."

"Not really," she said. "Not when you realize that we likely have an even bigger problem on our hands now." Appearing exhausted, she pushed herself to her feet and chucked the beer bottle into a bin.

"What do you mean?" I said, feeling the hair stand up on the back of my neck. "Why a bigger problem?"

"Do you have a twin by any chance?" she asked.

"No."

"Then we have a doppelgänger on our hands."

"That doesn't sound good."

"No," she said, "it's not good. It's very not good."

"What do we do?"

She leaned toward me over the table. "First thing we do is keep our mouths shut about it except to those who need to know. Doppelgängers cause a panic, and for good reason. Then, we gotta go trap this thing."

CHAPTER THIRTEEN

Nora knocked four times on Ruby's front door and tapped the toe of her boot as we waited.

I was gathering that this doppelgänger thing was a bigger deal than I'd originally feared.

My duplicate hadn't seemed dangerous when I'd met her, but Nora seemed to have had some sort of past brush with a doppelgänger that left her rattled.

She knocked four times again, harder.

The door cracked open, and Ruby's face poked through. "For fang's sake. What is it?" she hissed.

"We have a problem," said Nora.

Ruby blew a raspberry. "You *always* have a problem, dear. That's why I was hoping you'd go away rather than knock again."

"We need your help."

"You mean you want to make *your* problem *my* problem, and after eight pm. Have you no respect for age? I'm just a little old lady, and you pull me out of bed at all hours of the night to solve your problems?"

Nora didn't appear moved by the elderly act. "There's a doppelgänger in town."

Ruby cursed under her breath, and not an Eastwind idiom, but one from my old realm.

Wow, this *was* serious.

The white-haired witch opened the door wider and motioned us in.

The sound of footsteps padding down the stairs turned my head. Ezra appeared, not looking sleepy at all. "Visitors?"

"I knew you weren't already asleep," Nora said.

"I didn't say I was sleeping," Ruby countered. "I said I was in bed."

"What's going on?" Ezra asked.

Nora answered. "A doppelgänger is running around Eastwind, and Dahlia seems to be the first to have realized it."

"Roaring flame," he declared. "How long has it been since the last time?"

"A little over five years," Nora said.

"Not long enough," Ruby added. "Have you informed your husband yet?"

Nora shook her head. "This is the first place we came."

Ruby sighed. "That's probably just as well. If we can handle this ourselves, that would be ideal. Once the word gets around town that there's a doppelgänger, accusations have a way of flying, and all accountability goes out the window. It's suddenly, 'It was the doppelgänger who stole your potion, not me!' *The doppelgänger did this! The doppelgänger did that! You're not really her, you're a doppelgänger!*" She pressed her hands to the side of her head. "Absolutely intolerable."

"Hold on," I said, "does that mean that any of us could be a doppelgänger and not the real version?"

"It does," said Ezra with a sly smile. "Are you the doppelgänger or the real you?"

"The real me, of course!" I replied.

"Then I am, too," he said.

I understood his point. But it didn't mean I could know for certain who I was dealing with.

And suddenly I understood why having a doppelgänger roaming around town could cause such chaos.

"They can mimic what you look like, but they don't see inside your head," Nora explained. "They don't take on your history. So you can ask someone a question the doppelgänger wouldn't know the answer to, and that can help you figure it out."

"A question like what?" I asked.

"Where does Angelina work in New Orleans?"

"Ah. The South Wind."

"See? Ask me one."

I had to think about it. "What did Grim say to you the other day when you caught him with his paws up on the counter, eating your take-out?"

Nora grunted. "'I'm doing you a favor. You could stand to lose a few pounds.'"

Okay then. It was the real Nora.

She turned to Ruby, "What's your favorite ward on the ceiling?"

Ruby shuffled over a few steps and pointed up at a string of black pearls.

Nora nodded. "Checks out."

Finally, Ruby turned to Ezra. "What's your favorite part of my body?"

"Oh, come on," Nora said. "Do you two have to make everything weird?"

Ezra winked. "Your dimples."

Ruby nodded. "Yep. That's him."

Nora narrowed her eyes. "You don't have dimples, though."

"Not on my face, no."

Nora rolled her eyes, and I stifled a laugh.

The matter at hand was still serious business.

"We should keep it just the four of us for now," Ruby said. "If we can catch the doppelgänger, pin it down somehow without it changing into one of us and causing too much confusion, then we can call in Tanner."

"Why don't I just call him in now?" Nora asked.

Ruby frowned, tilting her head to the side. "Because you married a law-abiding man, Nora. You must learn his limitations." When Nora opened her mouth to protest, Ruby held up a hand and continued. "I get it. Gabby Bloom has been my dear friend for a long time. And the reason we can remain friends is *because* I don't tell her everything I get up to. That way, she doesn't have a legal imperative to stop me. She can simply turn a blind eye. Tanner deserves that luxury, too."

"Are we doing something illegal?" I asked.

"Only if we're lucky, dear." Ruby patted me on the shoulder then said, "I'd better get dressed. You too, Ezra. It's chilly outside, and that robe alone won't be enough to keep you warm."

Nora and I shared a glance, and then five minutes later, the four of us set out into the night to hunt down a doppelgänger.

CHAPTER FOURTEEN

I quickly learned there was an inherent problem built into finding someone who could look like anyone. The last I'd seen, she—they?—looked like me. I didn't like to think about what havoc the doppelgänger might be causing and blaming on me, but I also didn't like to think that the doppelgänger had already changed forms and might be anyone.

To avoid constantly having to ask each other questions every time we split up then came back together, the four of us decided on the code word "cucumber" to make sure we were speaking to the true version of the other.

It was late, so we set out for the place where most people who weren't already in bed went at this hour: Sheehan's Pub.

Two werewolves were sitting outside in the small patio area. Nora waved to them. "Hey, Hendrix. Running a bit behind tonight?"

He nodded. "I'll be over to Medium Rare before long. Treff here wanted to buy me another round first."

Nora nodded at the other man. "How's Ravi?"

He squinted at her. "You mean Raji?"

"Right, of course," she said. "Sorry, long day."

He waved her off. "I hear ya. She's fine. Learning to crawl. She'll be hunting in no time."

"Glad to hear it," Nora said. "You two have a good night." She turned to our group and muttered, "Not the doppelgänger."

"Who's Raji?" I asked.

"His daughter. He brings her into the diner almost every day."

"Ah. You didn't actually forget her name," I said.

Nora winked. "Just wanted to make sure *he* knew it."

As we stepped inside the pub, I was relieved to find that it wasn't overly crowded. A few tables had small groups seated at them, but thankfully, it wasn't a weekend. Otherwise, we would've been there all night asking people silly questions to verify identity.

Since Ezra and Nora were the two best-connected people of our group, both owning popular establishments that allowed them to interact with fellow Eastwinders daily, they made the rounds while Ruby and I settled in on stools at the bar.

Fiona Sheehan approached us on the other side of the long counter. "Miss True, you're not usually in here this late. Or ever."

"I'm not one for crowds, no."

"What brings you in?"

"I had a question for you, actually."

Fiona nodded. "Ask away."

"What's your father's middle name?"

"Stewart. Why do you ask?"

Ruby smiled. "I'm trying to keep my memory sharp in my old age. Wanted to test it against some trivia. Say, have you seen anyone acting strange today?"

Fiona appeared openly skeptical. "Acting strange in a bar? Yes, I can say I have."

"You know what I mean," Ruby said, "out of character."

Fiona chewed her bottom lip as she mulled it over. "No, I don't think so. Oh, wait. Count Malavic bought a round of drinks for everyone at lunchtime. He's not usually that generous."

Ruby waved it off. "He's up for re-election as Eastwind's treasurer next week."

"Right," Fiona said, nodding. "I didn't realize it was that time again. He does like to flaunt his wealth right before we vote. So then, I guess not. Everyone was their usual kind of strange today. Why do you ask? Something afoot?"

Ruby beamed. "There's always something afoot in Eastwind."

"True enough. Can I get you something to drink then?"

"No, we're just waiting on Nora and Ezra to finish chatting up everyone."

Fiona went back to wiping down the counter, and Ruby turned to me. "This might take a while."

But just as I was feeling the heaviness of our colossal task settle in, Nora strode over and said, "Paul Stormstruck said they had a strange encounter with Echo Chambers right before coming over here a half hour ago. Over by the entrance to the Parchment Catacombs."

"Strange?" Ruby asked.

Ezra was the one who answered. "He was wearing a

sweater from two seasons ago and smiling at the people who passed by."

"Goodness!" Ruby jumped down from the barstool. "That must be our doppelgänger."

Fiona popped her head up. "Did you just say 'doppelgänger'?"

"Of course not, dear." Ruby nodded toward the exit. "Shall we?"

———

Had I not been with Ruby, Ezra, and Nora, I might've felt antsy walking the streets at night, knowing that anyone could be the doppelgänger. But as it was, this was likely the safest place I could be right now. Neither Ruby nor Ezra had much regard for things like laws and norms, and both were powerful enough to do what it would take to make sure nothing happened to me.

"There he is," said Ezra, pointing down one of the streets to where the faun Echo Chambers was strolling away from us. I remembered the haughty way he'd carried himself at the Blue Sky parade, all confidence and trendiness. It wasn't just there that he conducted himself in that regard. Echo liked to wear fabrics that caught the eye—gold silks, bright frills, that sort of thing—any time he stepped outside his front door. Indeed, I couldn't imagine him being caught dead in the hand-knit sweater he was currently sporting, whose colors ranged from dry clay to wet clay.

"You're right," Ruby said, "that sweater is as unfashionable as they come. Echo would gallop into a dragon's open mouth before wearing that around. The doppelgänger must not have done its research."

"We need to check on Echo once this is all over, too," Nora said. "Make sure he's not being kept prisoner in a basement somewhere."

I whipped my head toward her. "Is that what they do?"

She let out a big exhale. "If necessary to keep up the facade, yes. Having both the real person and the doppelgänger around ruins the illusion they're trying to create."

"I didn't realize how close I was to danger," I muttered. But still, the mirror of me that I'd encountered in that side street earlier that evening hadn't tried to kidnap me. She hadn't seemed aggressive at all, other than the fact that she had assaulted Dante. So, perhaps I should say that she didn't seem aggressive *toward me*. She quite seemed like she was on my team, if nothing else.

That wasn't lining up with the description of a doppelgänger that I was getting from the others at all.

"Hey!" Nora called. "Echo!"

The faun turned around, spotted us, and smiled broadly. "Well, hello there!"

"Never seen a doppelgänger do such a poor impression of the real thing," Ruby muttered.

Echo clip-clopped over to us, waving. "Three Fifth Winds and a South Wind wandering around at night? Sounds like quite an adventure is ahoof!"

He wouldn't stop grinning as he came within a few yards of us. I had no idea he could offer such a pleasant smile. I'd never seen it from him.

Ezra inched around the side of Echo, beginning to cut off his route of escape.

I wasn't a fan of the idea that the doppelgänger might sprint my way and I'd be in charge of catching him. But what was I hoping for, that he'd charge toward Ruby? She was much older than I was. I wasn't tall or particularly strong, but I still had youth on my side to some extent.

"We know what you are," Nora said, catching and holding Echo's gaze.

"What do you mean, 'what you are'? I'm Echo. I'm in a great mood. I'm feeling a spirit of generosity toward my fellow living beings. I'm even thinking about donating to Miss Clementine's animal sanctuary. How much do you think she'd need to be able to feed all the animals for a year? I bet I have that in leprechaun gold alone. You can't take it with you, you know. Wealth, I mean. Might as well leave behind a legacy of giving."

"You might be the worst impersonator I've ever met," Ruby said.

Echo appeared genuinely wounded. "Impersonator? Me? What are you talking about?"

"You're not Echo," Ruby said.

"But I am! I'm absolutely Echo. What makes you think I'm not?"

Ezra was the one who answered. "Echo wouldn't be caught dead in that sweater."

Echo pouted his bottom lip. "But Echo loves this sweater."

"If you're really him," Ezra countered, "why are you referring to yourself in the third person?"

Echo shrugged.

Pulling out his wand, Ezra said, "We know you're a doppelgänger. If you give yourself up, we won't hurt you. But you're not welcome in Eastwind. Your kind have caused way too much trouble."

Echo said nothing. Instead, he stared deeply at Ezra, cocking his head to the side as if solving a riddle. "I'm not a doppelgänger. And *you* are not that young." And then Echo began to change, and as he did so, his sweater changed with him.

I looked to Nora for some direction, but she was holding steady, pointedly observing what was unfolding before her.

As long as Nora wasn't running away, I supposed I could stick around and see what happened.

The being's skin darkened, and the oversized sweater transformed into an outfit I was already familiar with because it was the exact same one Ezra had changed into earlier.

"Siren's song," Ruby muttered. "Ezra, that's..."

She didn't have to say. It was clear enough who the doppelgänger now resembled. It was Ezra, but not him as he appeared just then. Instead, the doppelgänger was a version of Ezra who'd aged along with Ruby.

The real Ezra made a pained and feral noise, then charged toward the imposter.

I had a strange impulse to step in—after all, he was about to beat up an old man—but my feet were glued to the cobblestones below them. All of this was simply too weird to know what action to take.

Nora knew what to do, though, and she darted forward, though whether she was attempting to intervene to prevent Ezra from tackling the doppelgänger or trying to help him do it was yet unclear.

It didn't matter in the end, because Ezra beat her to the punch. He leaped, a snarl on his face. I'd never seen the South Wind look so fierce. I expected his pyromancy powers to flash before me at any moment, but he seemed too enraged to even remember he had them. He was ready for a good old-fashioned throwdown, instead.

I gritted my teeth, bracing for the impact of the two Ezras colliding, tumbling to the ground with a crunch of bodies. But only one Ezra hit the ground with a crunch. The young one. He'd passed straight through the older version.

"Sweet baby jackalope!" Nora shouted, pulling up short and staring at Old Ezra with wide eyes. She looked from it to the young Ezra on the ground then back again.

Time seemed to freeze in that instant while everyone absorbed the unexpected development.

Everyone except for the Old Ezra Ares.

"What in the realm are you?" Nora breathed.

Instead of answering, the being took off down the alley at a speed that didn't match its aged appearance. It disappeared around a corner, and only once it was out of sight did I remember that my lungs needed air.

"Sooo... not a doppelgänger," said Nora, staring after where it'd just vanished.

"Then what is it?" I asked.

She shook her head, totally at a loss.

Ruby helped a shaken Ezra off the ground and dusted off the back of his shirt. "I think that's enough excitement for us for tonight, don't you?"

Ezra's eyes were wide as a spooked deer's. He looked like he'd seen a ghost. And considering what I'd just witnessed, I couldn't entirely rule that out.

"Good thing the library stays open all night," Nora said.

"Ooh! We're going?" I asked. As soon as I heard the excitement in my voice, I knew that it didn't match the somber tone of the moment. I cleared my throat and made sure to act a little less excited.

"Unless Ruby or Ezra know what all that was?" She turned her attention to Ruby.

"Goddess, no," Ruby replied. "I haven't a clue. Well, I have, but nothing I can come up with is any less trouble than a doppelgänger, so I don't want to jinx us by saying."

"Agreed," Ezra replied shakily.

Ruby looked him up and down, concern carving deep lines in her forehead. "We'd better get you home."

"Fine," Nora said. "Y'all do that, and Dahlia and I can search the library for any hint at what we're dealing with. Doesn't look like there's any sense in hunting this thing until we know what it is."

"There may not be sense in hunting it even when you *do* know what it is," Ruby added.

"If you need help, might be time to call in the officials. Gabby's golden cuffs can attach to just about anything, corporeal or not."

I'd seen those cuffs come out. The angel sheriff shot them at whoever deserved to take a breather. She had great aim, too. The idea of getting her involved made everything seem a little more manageable. But first, we needed to figure out what the heck was going on.

Ruby kept an arm around Ezra's waist as she guided him back toward his house.

"You know," I heard her murmur, "you age excellently. If that version of you were to show up at my door some evening, I'd let him in."

Nora and I looked at each other. She'd overheard it, too. But instead of commenting, she said, "To the library?"

CHAPTER FIFTEEN

I was so glad to have an excuse to finally visit the Eastwind Library. It was a magical place, both literally and figuratively.

In the literal sense, the magic was immediately obvious. Not only could I feel it on my skin the second we climbed the stairs out front and entered the giant stone building, but the place was full of ghosts who were somehow able to carry books around with them. Usually, spirits couldn't pull off a feat like that, but it seemed that it was possible within the walls of the library. I couldn't blame them for haunting this place. If I were unfortunate enough to come back as a ghost, this would be my hangout, too, most likely. So many books I wanted to read and so little time! But if I had zero responsibilities and all the time I wanted? Yes, definitely the library.

And figuratively the place was magical because it was full of books. Anywhere this full of stories and knowledge was magic.

"The ghosts really come out at night," Nora said as we

crossed the main reading area, "when it's not as busy with the living."

"Are they scared of the living?" I asked.

Nora laughed. "Not at all. But if you've ever walked through one, you know it's like walking under a freezing waterfall. The librarians get complaints, because it's hard to avoid ghosts when you can't see them. Nothing will pull you out of a story quicker than a ghost absentmindedly walking straight through you. So, the librarians limit the number who can be in the main lobby during the day."

"And where do the rest of the ghosts go when they're not here?"

"Either into the lesser used tunnels or... wherever ghosts go between appearances. An in-between space, but I don't know that it can really be described accurately with words."

An elf looked up at us from where she sat behind the librarian's desk, completing what appeared to be a crossword.

Nora waved to her as we passed.

"You're here late," the elf replied. "Investigating something?"

"How'd you guess?"

"You know where to find what you need?"

"Generally speaking, yes," Nora said. "I'll let you know if I'm wrong."

The elf returned to her crossword, and Nora added, "That's Helena. Don't let her fool you; she's quite friendly when it comes time to talk about specific books."

I spotted Anton, the ogre who cooked up the most amazing meals at Medium Rare. He was settled in at one of the wooden reading tables, attention buried deep in the massive tome open on the table before him.

Nora patted Anton on the shoulder as we passed him, and he didn't look up.

"You coming to work tomorrow?" she asked.

"No. Day off," he grunted.

Once we were far enough away to not be overheard, she whispered, "Not an imposter."

I tossed another glance at his hulking frame. Not exactly intimidating when it was hunched over a book, but definitely not one I would want to try to capture. "Sure glad of that."

I let my gaze roam the tall, packed bookshelves that we passed, took fleeting notice of the various spirits browsing the stacks or sitting cross-legged on the floor with a book open in front of them. The ghosts were a comfort, frankly. I was pretty sure that whatever this shapeshifting thing was, it couldn't pull off the shimmering form of a ghost. Ergo, as long as I was surrounded by ghosts, I was *not* worried that one of them was an imposter.

"Let's see if I can remember the way through the tunnels," Nora said. "I think I lucked out the last time I came this way, when I was trying to figure out what the wraith was. Only got lost back here for a few minutes before I righted myself."

I tried not to let my excitement show that I would get to experience the tunnels I'd heard so much about from Grace.

As we made our way down a set of carved stone stairs, the open airiness of the main part of the library contracted as the low ceilings and narrow walls surrounded us. We were heading underground.

Torches floating overhead lit our way as I followed Nora, hoping she *did* remember where she was going. While it was a lovely novelty to be down here, with the rough walls on either side and the time-worn stone beneath my feet, it was *not* somewhere I would want to get lost in. I wasn't claustrophobic—quite the opposite, since I loved feeling tucked away—but I could definitely see the appeal wearing off before too long.

We passed arches that led to rooms full of old books or even more hallways, and I quickly lost track of our route. Best to make sure I didn't get separated from Nora. I shuddered to think what it would be like if that were to happen. Did the library have some sort of rescue plan in place for browsers who went missing?

"Here we go," Nora said.

The room we entered felt more like a wine cellar than a library section with the cold air and stillness that came with being who-knows how far underground. She led me to a long row of books. "The A's start here. This section contains information about every type of creature or entity that's ever been catalogued by Eastwinders."

I decided not to ask what would happen if what we were dealing with had never been catalogued before? What if it was some new danger? There was a first time for everything, after all.

I stared down the long row. Easily a thousand books lay before me. "We have to browse all of these?" I asked.

"Thankfully, no. You'll be able to rule a lot out right away. For instance, we're not dealing with an angel or an archetype."

"What's an archetype? I mean, I think I know..."

"It's not what you're thinking. It's something else.

Something that's possibly an even bigger pain in the hide than doppelgängers. But I can rule it out just from what I know of the situation. You can just skip over anything you recognize and ask me if you're not sure. But also, it's not just this row we need to search. It's the next five."

I rubbed at my eyes without even thinking about it. "Does the library provide coffee?"

"I wish. If you start falling asleep, try thinking back to the moment you saw Ezra dive through his older self. That might wake you up."

"True," I said, replaying it in my head. "That was a real shock."

"And if you do fall asleep, we can take a break and get some coffee."

Nora woke me with a gentle shake of my shoulder. I blinked away the vivid dream I was having and struggled to orient myself in my surroundings. Where was I? Definitely not my bedroom.

Oh right. The library.

The book I'd been browsing was open in my lap as I slumped against one of the cold stone walls of the quiet room. "Coffee break," Nora said.

I nodded, looked down at my book, remembered that I was only to B in the alphabet. "How long was I asleep?"

"Not sure," Nora said, "I dozed off myself reading about *bannicks*. Pretty sure it's not that."

I remembered the dream I'd just been having. I was at Stews and Brews, standing by the table where Dante and Izzy were having a romantic dinner and absolutely letting him have it. The memory of the dream was unsettling. I didn't know I could be that angry in my dreams. It was me yelling at them, but not me. I was yelling at him in a way that was over-the-top, illogical, designed to hurt.

"You okay?" she asked, staring at me with concern.

"Yeah, just remembering a dream I had."

Her brows shot up. "Do tell?"

I shrugged. "It was just a dream."

"Noooo." She shook her head. "Not with us. I mean, sure, sometimes a dream is just a dream, but for Fifth Winds, a dream is often something much more important."

"Really?"

She nodded. "And I don't know about you, but I'd welcome any hint that might mean skipping over the rest of these books."

"Okay, well, I was dreaming that I was confronting Dante at his dinner with Izzy." I paused, a strange hint of something forming in my subconscious, just out of reach.

"Go on."

"I was yelling at him, absolutely laying into him. And I... I slapped him."

"And did it feel real? Did you feel your hand make contact?"

"No. Before it did, you woke me up."

She grimaced. "Sorry about that. I would've let you slap him first, if I'd known." She paused. "Are you *sure* it wasn't you at the restaurant? With the dream you just had, and the way he was acting... Maybe you were sleepwalking after all? Maybe your dream was more of a memory, and you got to act out your fantasy. Reading a man his rights after he's been hot and cold with you does sound like some sort of wish fulfillment. If Tanner ever acted that way—"

"What did you say?" I asked, my breath catching in my chest.

She looked at me curiously. "If Tanner ever—"

"No, before that."

She had to think about it. "Sounds like wish fulfillment?"

That was it. That was what we were looking for. "Sweet baby jackalope," I breathed. "No, it couldn't be. He couldn't have thought I was *serious*."

"What? Who?"

I looked her dead in the eyes. "Nora, do genies actually grant wishes?"

CHAPTER SIXTEEN

As soon as Nora showed me the way back into the main section of the library, I was off, power walking out of there, a witch on a mission.

"Where are you going?" she asked, jogging to catch up. "And why?"

"I need to find Liberty Freeman. He owes me an explanation."

The sky was still dark as I stepped out of the library and started down the stairs, Nora following behind me.

"Okay, one more question," she said. "Do you know where he lives?"

"Oh." I paused with one foot in the air. "No. Do you?"

"Yep. You're not the first person to need to track him down at his house for genie shenanigans. I'm sure you won't be the last, either. Follow me."

As we walked, our brisk pace helping to keep me warm in the pre-dawn cold, I explained my theory to her in greater detail. She only had a few questions before her curiosity was satisfied, and she concluded with, "You couldn't have known. *He* should've known better, though."

The streets were empty. Not even the early vendors were setting up yet. I had no idea what time it was until we passed the clock tower in the middle of the Emporium. Just after four in the morning. I hadn't gotten that coffee she'd mentioned, but the cold and my simmering anger were enough to keep me alert now.

Nora was right. Liberty Freeman should've known better. At the very least, he could've warned me. His unwanted "help," if that's what it was, had likely cost me any chance of a future with Dante. And if I didn't somehow put a stop to whatever that imposter was, who knew what kind of chaos might erupt in town. How dare he!

I only vaguely mused at the unusual amount of anger I was allowing in, and all directed at Liberty. It felt good. Right. Useful. Maybe this was how Dante had felt when he chewed me out.

Remembering the way that confrontation had left me feeling only caused me to pick up the pace. Oh yeah, I had a few things to say to the meddling genie.

Because the streets were so desolate at this hour, I noticed the sound of an additional pair of boots on the ground immediately. So did Nora. We both turned toward the source of the footsteps.

I was pretty sure that no matter how many times I saw myself appear, I'd never fully get used to it. She appeared out of an alley, stepping into a small patch of streetlight. She still had my coat, which, yeah, was a good purchase. It complemented my skin tone.

Focus, Dahlia!

The thing—not a doppelgänger, but some other entity most likely conjured by genie powers—looked like me again. Not just the same coat, but the same hair, pants, and boots. I suspected it probably also had a small scar on the back of its right thigh, though it had never personally been sliced up while hopping a chain-link fence to escape an attack chihuahua. Whatever that thing was, it didn't have the experience I had, only the image. And perhaps something else of mine, something I didn't know how to name yet...

"Uh, code word?" Nora muttered.

"Cucumber," I whispered back, covering my mouth with a flat hand.

The being approached us.

"What do you want?" Nora asked.

Imposter Me grinned innocently and shrugged. "Just curious where you're going. Not a lot going on right now around town. I was starting to get bored. I saw your husband earlier, though. Thought about turning into you and committing some crimes, but it didn't feel right."

"You have a conscience now?" I demanded, letting my anger at Liberty spill over.

Imposter Me pouted her lips and shook her head. "No, not exactly. More like it didn't seem true to her." She nodded toward Nora. "And I got the sense Tanner would let a petty crime slide anyway, if his precious wife was the culprit."

"You could do whatever you wanted," Nora said. "There's nothing you could do while pretending to be me that would hurt my relationship with Tanner."

The being's eyes—my eyes—flickered to me. "What about yelling at him in public?"

Nora laughed. "He'd probably like it. Listen, we don't have time for your games. We're gonna put an end to this."

The being's eyes lit up. "Are you really? Can I come?"

Nora shrugged her off and motioned for us to get on our way again. "I don't know how to stop you from it."

The being pumped her fist. "Perfect. Let's go! I can't wait to see what Liberty has to say."

Nora and I exchanged a quick glance. Neither one of us had said who we were going to see. At least my suspicion about who was responsible for this—and who could possibly put an end to it—was all but confirmed.

The being skipped along beside us as we continued toward Liberty's house.

"Why were you trying to get into the studio the other night?" I asked.

"Isn't it obvious?"

Once I paused to think about it, it was. "You wanted to leave a dead animal for me."

She looked genuinely surprised and stopped skipping. "A *what*?"

"A dead animal," I said. "You're the one who's been leaving them, aren't you?"

"You think I'm some kind of lunatic?"

I shrugged. "You could be. I don't know what you are yet."

She started skipping again. "No, it wasn't that."

"Then what was it?"

She grinned at me. "I had a feeling you were heading there that morning, and I wanted to meet you."

Whatever that feeling was, she'd been right, but the timing had been off by about thirty seconds, which was why I'd been able to follow her there.

I never would've found Liberty's home without Nora, that's for sure. It was easy to overlook and not exactly a house by any visible standards. Instead, there was simply an average-looking door standing alone in the middle of an empty field on the edge of town.

"Do I... knock?" I asked, staring at it.

"I don't think you'll have to."

As soon as she said it, the door swung open.

"Come on in." I recognized Liberty's voice, but it sounded both far away and right in front of me.

What appeared on the other side of the door was utterly baffling to my brain. Not the continuation of the field in which I stood, but a massive entryway with marble floors. No matter how much I told myself that there was magic beyond my imagination in Eastwind, knowing that theoretically and actually witnessing it with my own eyes were two different things.

I started forward but realized only one person was following me. I looked back at Nora. "What is it? You're coming, right?"

"I think you should go in by yourself," she said.

"What? Why?" I wasn't big on the idea of going alone, just me and this being Liberty had conjured, walking into his strange house.

"Just a little bit of Insight."

I wanted to argue, but she'd told me enough about her powers for me to know that when her Insight spoke up, that was the end of the discussion for her. And it was usually onto something no amount of thinking could touch.

"If you're nervous," she added, "remember why you're here. What trouble he's caused you. It's okay to get angry when someone's wronged you."

"I'm starting to think you're right about that." I recalled the memory of Dante's anger as he'd confronted me in the shop. He'd been right to be angry, at least based on what he thought had happened. And I'd been right to be hurt and a little scared. None of this was my fault. Sure, I may have accidentally wished it into existence, but I couldn't have known what I'd done!

Liberty knew, though.

I used that anger to unglue my feet and march through the open door ahead of me.

"What are you going to say to him?" my duplicate asked, hardly hiding her excitement.

"Hush," I snapped. "I've heard enough out of you." The order shocked even me. I'd never spoken to someone like that in my *life*.

It actually felt pretty good.

The entry hall of Liberty's home could only be described as cavernous. Impossibly high vaulted ceilings towered over a manufactured tropical paradise.

The violet and white tiles on the floor were laid out in a checkerboard pattern, and ahead of me was a massive circular fountain that shot glittering gold tendrils rather than water. I could've sworn I saw a dolphin quickly leap out of the gold surface, but maybe it was a trick of the light. On either side of me were long rectangular slabs of some pitch-black stone with a wall of water shooting up from the center of them. I wasn't sure where to go from there, but no sooner had I realized that than the tile in front of me lit up. I stepped onto it and the light disappeared, then the next tile ahead lit up. I was being shown the way.

Following the pattern, I circled around the fountain in the center and continued straight toward two large staircases branching off in opposite directions. Between them was a hallway that sloped downward and disappeared out of sight. The lights on the floor took me into the hallway.

I tried to stay focused on my mission and not get distracted by the vibrant paintings on the wall depicting jovial gatherings—feasts, parties, celebrations—where the subjects danced and swayed in the frames. Could I have stared at the canvases all day? Sure, if I had nothing better to do.

I forced myself to follow Nora's advice and remember the mess that had led me to this point, a mess that Liberty had likely orchestrated. By the time the tiles led me to an open door through which I found the genie lounging in a hammock tied between two palm trees in a tropical paradise, I was ready to give him a piece of my mind. At least I'd *thought* I was. The sudden appearance of the outdoor scene indoors threw me for a bit of a loop.

But when my duplicate said, "Ooh!" and rushed past me to a small tiki bar in the white sand where she began mixing herself a drink, I remembered my business.

Liberty smiled at me from his hammock. Above us, the sun shone, warm and inviting. I stepped off the tile and into the soft sand as he spread his arms in a gesture of welcome. "Dahlia. So good to see you."

I opened my mouth to say what I wanted to say, but he interrupted me.

"You might want to take off your boots. The sand has a way of getting in there and staying."

I thought about ignoring his advice—after all, I was mad at him, wasn't I? —but who wants sand in their boots? I kicked them off, along with my thick socks, and set them out in the hallway.

"Liberty, I—"

"There's a coatrack just behind you, if you get hot."

I spotted the coatrack next to the wall, its legs buried in a sand drift. Yes, I supposed I was a little toasty in the warm sunshine.

I hung up my coat, shoved the sleeves of my sweater up my forearms, and said, "Enough! You know what you did."

He grinned and his attention shifted to the duplicate of me who was still wearing her coat and boots. "You don't like her?"

"Of course I don't! She ruined my relationship with Dante!"

"Ah." He pulled a creamy frozen drink with a small pink umbrella out of thin air and took a sip through a striped straw. "You think *she* ruined the relationship."

"Yes." I hoped I wouldn't have to catch him up on all the events. It would take so much time that I might lose the momentum of all the outrage I'd mustered.

He didn't ask for clarification, though. Instead, he replied, "But she's *you*."

"No, she's not. She can't be. *I'm* me. I'm Dahlia Wildes!"

He wagged a finger at me. "You are. But there's a part of you—quite a few parts of you—that you've tucked away. You said as much to me after the Blue Sky feast."

"I *never* would've chewed out Dante in a restaurant," I replied. "That wasn't me. That was her."

"You sure about that?"

I was quite new to this whole anger thing, and it felt like it was getting the best of me. My brain was starting to feel fuzzy. When I opened my mouth to respond, I couldn't form the words. Too many wanted to spill out, and some of them were especially unkind.

Liberty sat up in his hammock and swung his feet around, digging his toes into the sand. "Look, we all have parts of ourselves we keep locked up. Sometimes that's a good thing. That part of us who wants to murder everyone who inconveniences us? Sure, keep that one tucked away. But we go overboard. The way you're feeling right now, the anger you feel toward me—it's novel to you, isn't it? You're not used to it."

He seemed to be waiting for a response, but I said nothing, so he prompted, "Am I wrong? Have you been telling people off left and right and I somehow haven't heard about it through the Eastwind rumor mill?" He was suppressing a smile, but poorly. I didn't happen to find any of this humorous.

"You're right," I said. "I don't get angry much. Something about a genie meddling in my love life really ticks me off, though."

"Certainly this isn't the first time in your life when someone did something where this anger might've been useful for you, when anger could've helped you stand up for yourself like you're doing right now? Don't you see, Dahlia? She"—he nodded toward the duplicate— "is *that* part of you."

I looked over at her. She was finishing the first drink she'd made for herself, chugging down the last of it before tossing the empty glass over her shoulder, where it landed silently in the soft sand. She finished off the display with a loud belch.

"I'm not saying it's a bad idea to tone down some of those parts of yourself sometimes," Liberty conceded, "but

I've been watching you since you came to Eastwind. You're nice. Nobody has an unkind word to say about you. And you work harder than almost anyone else in town. You don't get paid enough at the studio to keep you and your familiar comfortably fed, and Nora drags you around to work homicide investigations with no promise of payment for the time you spend. It's not just your love life where you're burying your needs, Dahlia."

"You've been watching me that closely?"

He shrugged. "Why not? Being immortal is living in tedium. You're the newest person in Eastwind, and I appreciate the novelty. Plus, you're more interesting than you give yourself credit for."

"So you conjured her for, what, a little extra drama to keep your telenovela interesting? This is my life, Liberty, it's not meant for your entertainment."

"You said she yelled at Dante," he continued, keeping his part in the conversation lighthearted. "That means a part of *you* wanted to yell at him. Part of you was angry. Part of you felt like you were getting walked all over. When you wished you could stand up for yourself, I granted that wish by bringing that hidden part of you into existence, so you could start granting *your own wishes*."

"I didn't want to shout at him!" I insisted.

"Oh stop," he said, waving off my protest. "Of course you did. Your shade wouldn't have done it if a part of you hadn't wanted it."

"My shade? Is that what she is?" I asked. Liberty nodded, smiling pleasantly. *Sheesh,* I thought, *it would've been years until we made it to the Ss in that section of the library.* "Is that, like, a ghost?"

"No, though I have heard ghosts called that before.

She's a shade of *you*. A color of your spectrum that you won't let shine."

"For good reason," I said. "Liberty, you can't just go around hitting people and not expect consequences."

"Couldn't agree more," he said. "But does hiding away the part of you who fights for what your heart wants not *also* come with consequences?"

That made me pause and think. He wasn't wrong. The consequences of not being honest—with myself or with Dante—about how I wanted us to be exclusive and committed had led to him spending all that time with Izzy. It'd also led to me feeling, well, crummy about myself. "Fang's sake, Liberty," I snapped, struggling to stay furious with him.

The shade of me leaned her head back and belched. "That's a damned good drink."

"Help yourself to another," Liberty replied, before returning to our conversation. "The thing about shades is that they don't get into quite so much trouble if we allow ourselves to get into a little bit of it first. They don't go too far toward, say, aggression if we're not already too far in the other direction."

"You're telling me I'm *responsible* for her actions?"

"In a way, yes. Because you're responsible for you. And she reflects a part of you."

I gave in and considered it. "She didn't just look like me the whole time, though. She looked like Echo Chambers and Ezra Ares, too. Maybe more people who I didn't see."

"A shade can reflect the hidden parts of whoever it chooses."

That made sense enough, and I was happy for a break

from reflecting on my own situation. "It turned into Echo in an unfashionable but comfortable sweater," I said.

Liberty threw his head back and laughed, a deep booming sound. "Of course that's what he keeps out of sight."

"And Ezra was... old."

Liberty nodded. "Yes, that adds up, too."

It certainly did. But I still wasn't a fan of the fact that the part of myself I was hiding away wanted to accost someone.

"Do you still wish you knew how to stand up for yourself?" he asked, a sly smile turning his lips. "Or do you need to yell at me some more first?"

I cringed. "I guess I'm all set."

"I would say so. Here you are, stomping into the home of the most powerful being in Eastwind, telling him what you really think. Sounds like the shade's job is complete." He snapped his fingers, and my duplicate disappeared with her half-finished drink still in hand.

"You didn't even let her finish?" I said. "Kind of rude."

He chuckled. "She's not real, Dahlia."

"Oh right." I looked down at my feet in the sand. The sun sure felt nice, but it was clear my job here was done. "I guess I'd better, uh..."

I grabbed my coat from the hanger and dusted my feet off before I stepped back onto the checkerboard tile of the hallway.

"There is one more lingering question you haven't had answered yet," he added.

I turned back toward him. "There is?" I had no doubt I would think of a thousand more questions about this situation the moment I stepped outside of his house and it was too late to turn around and demand answers. That was just how my brain worked. It always thought of the right question to ask about ten minutes too late. Just then, however, I had no idea what question I'd missed.

Instead of answering me directly, he said, "Here, take this," and pulled from the air a small metal disk, which he tossed my way. I nearly fumbled it but managed to hold on. It was a small, flat can.

As I puzzled over it, he said, "Open that up and set it out in the Time to Kiln studio. Then keep an eye on it."

Ah, right. Interesting.

I considered asking him how he knew about my situation with the dead animals in the studio, but this was Liberty Freeman we were talking about. Might as well ask why rain was wet. It just was, and he just knew.

"Thanks," I said. "I'll do that."

"Are you still angry with me?" he asked playfully.

"I am," I said. "But I think I'll just let you know that now so I don't have to deck you at the next town festival."

Liberty guffawed. "Fair enough. I'm sorry you didn't like how we got to this point, but I'm glad we got here."

"Easy for you to say. You're not the one who owes Dante a dragon-size apology for something you only kinda did."

"So you *do* plan on owning up to it. Glad to hear it." He offered me one last friendly wave as I tucked the can into my coat pocket and picked up my boots and socks. I didn't pause to put them on but carried them with me instead. I had a sudden urge to get back out into the open air, even if it meant enduring the cold wind instead of enjoying the warm sun.

CHAPTER SEVENTEEN

If I thought confronting a genie was scary, I had no idea how fast my heart would race thinking about what I ought to do next. It scared the dickens out of me to even consider it, but I'd heard Liberty loud and clear. I didn't need another nudge to learn the lesson I was supposed to gain from the trouble with that shade.

And yet, as soon as I was out in the cold again, no longer facing down a powerful magical being, my brain immediately began concocting a million reasons why it wasn't necessary to speak with Dante, why it would actually be better if I didn't, if I gave him his space, let him cool down and see if he came back around. If he never did, then I was never that important to him, right? Why go through a confrontation like I was sure we'd have if I dropped in on him when I was nobody special to him?

Nora appeared by my side. "You survived."

"I'm... did you think I wasn't going to make it out of there alive?"

"No, I figured you would, but there's always that little voice that wonders."

"I thought you would've gone home," I said.

"Nah, I wanted to make sure you survived. What are friends for, right?" She paused, frowning at me. "I see the double is gone. Thought you'd be more excited about that."

"It was a shade," I said. "A part of us we hide away."

She looked me up and down. "Oh yeah? You've been hiding a feisty fighter in you this whole time? I didn't know you had all that in you."

"I didn't either. But now I do."

"Good. That sounds like someone I'd like to take down to Sheehan's on a Friday night. Maybe get into some trouble."

"Is *everyone* in this town bored out of their minds and looking for drama?" I asked.

She shrugged. "When there's not an unsolved murder, yeah. Pretty much."

I felt suddenly exhausted and hugged my coat tighter around me.

"Ready to head home and get some sleep?" she asked.

Every bone in my body ached for sleep. But I could already see how things would go if I went back to the house with her. I would sleep like the dead, sure, but when I woke up, I just had this feeling it would be the old Dahlia who started the next day. The one who needed Liberty to conjure a nuisance of a shade just to figure out what she wanted.

But if I could keep going at this point, push ahead, something inside me knew that the hard lesson I learned just might stick. And if it did, I might save myself the trouble of having to learn it all over again. Two options, the outcome of each clear as a blue sky to me.

The image appeared in my mind of Atlas sleeping soundly on the bed at that very moment, warm and cuddly, taking up so much of the bed that I would have to snuggle up close to claim a spot. Atlas would understand if I skipped out on speaking to the man who'd yelled at me not even a week before.

Wouldn't he?

"I'm definitely ready to go to the house and get in bed," I said. "But there's something I have to do first."

Nora cocked her head to the side. "Yeah?"

"I need to sort things out with Dante. Apologize to him."

"For what? You didn't yell at him at Stews and Brews."

"But I did," I said. "Maybe not in the most literal sense, but I caused all of that because I wasn't brave enough to ask myself how much he meant to me and what I wanted from the relationship. So when he asked me what I wanted, I didn't know. It's nobody else's responsibility to know what I want but mine."

"Okay," she said, slowly nodding. "If that's what you want to do."

I groaned. "It's not what I want to do *at all*."

"But you're going to do it anyway."

"Exactly. Because it's fighting for what I do want, which is Dante."

"Right." She clapped me on the shoulder. "Do you need backup?"

"Thank you, but no. I think I need to do this on—"

"Phew! Great. Because if I go any longer without sleep,

Ted's gonna show up looking for a client." Without another word, she peeled off in the direction of her house.

It was just me now. No Atlas, no Nora, no shade. If I wanted things to be better with Dante, I had to make them that way.

I turned toward Dante's apartment. It was still far too early for him to be up for work, since Franco's Pizza didn't open for another handful of hours. Would he be even more angry if I woke him up?

I passed the clock tower as I passed through the Emporium. Only five thirty in the morning.

Okay, maybe waking him up wasn't the best move. But going to sleep wasn't either.

Oh, I was terrible when it came to decisions like this. Should I wait? Would I lose this momentum if I did?

I was surprised when a soft voice inside of me whispered, *It's not momentum carrying you. It's something deeper.*

I'd heard that voice a few times before, and every time it had spoken to me, it'd been right. Maybe I should simply trust it. After all, it didn't feel like momentum alone was what kept me putting one foot in front of the other on the way to his apartment. Instead, it felt like something had shifted. I didn't want to confront Dante and risk him yelling at me all over again, but I did want things to be better between us, and this was the only way.

I wouldn't go home, but I also didn't have to stomp straight there. It was too early for Dante to be up, but there were plenty of early risers around town, including Henry Hardtimes. A New Leaf, which he owned, opened at five every morning. I was definitely overdue for some coffee. Maybe even a chocolate croissant. But then I remembered that I was down to my last few coins before my next payday. Not even enough to buy the coffee, most likely.

I wish I had just a little more, I thought as I slipped my hand into my coat pocket, feeling around for the coins.

Next to the can Liberty had given me, my fingertips felt the rough surface of heavy coins. Not the small, smooth copper ones, either. I pulled the coins out of my pocket. They were gold. Plenty to buy all the coffee and croissants I could want for the rest of the week, at least.

"Okay, then, Liberty," I said. "I'm learning to spot a hint when I see it."

CHAPTER EIGHTEEN

Dante's apartment was on the bottom floor of a two-story brick building a few blocks from Fulcrum Park. Even with my much-needed diversion to A New Leaf for a pick-me-up, his shift at Franco's Pizza was still hours off. I was worried that he wouldn't be up yet, that I would wake him up from a dead sleep when I knocked and would have to break through the haze of interrupted dreaming to get through to him.

But when I approached his building, the first glow of dawn nudging its way down the cobblestone street, I saw that there was already a light on inside his unit. I blushed slightly, realizing that it was coming from behind the curtains of his bedroom window, and that meant I was familiar enough with the layout of his apartment to recognize such a thing. Yes, I was nearly thirty, and it still made me feel girlish and a little bit rebellious to have been in a boy's room. Unsupervised, no less!

Dante wasn't a boy, though. He was a man. And I was a

woman. A woman who owed the man not only an explanation, but an apology.

But then it occurred to me: what if he wasn't alone?

My lungs turned to bricks and dropped into my feet at the possibility. I hadn't spoken to him since he yelled at me. What had happened in his life in the time since that happened? Had he written me off completely and then...

I wanted to throw up even thinking about it. But there was no denying it. Izzy could be in his apartment at that very minute, and not getting an early start, but rather not having yet slept. I felt my face warm with anticipatory humiliation. What if I knocked on his door to apologize and she answered? She was probably thrilled that I'd accosted him at the restaurant. It meant he was all hers now. Had he ranted to her about me over the last couple of days? Had they bonded over the event?

A sharp pain was forming behind my eyes. *I should go home,* I thought. *This was a stupid idea. Of course he's moved on. She's prettier than me, friendlier than me, more interesting than me. He deserves someone like that. Just let it go, Dahlia. He's likely moved on, and you should too.*

I didn't turn to leave, though. Staring at the light filtering through the curtains of his bedroom window, I wanted nothing more than to turn around and not have to face this possible humiliation, not subject myself to being yelled at all over again by Dante or subtly poked at by Izzy. I realized, though, that I owed him an apology whether he ended up choosing me or not. I cared about him, as much as it hurt me to think about it in that moment; and because I did, I owed it to him to endure whatever he had to throw at me. I'd earned it, after all, even if I never would've actually done what the shade did. She was a part of me I had to own.

I could've stood there, putting off the encounter for all of eternity, but miraculously something inside me lifted my left boot off the cobblestones below it. One step, then another, and suddenly I was standing on his doorstep. Rolling my shoulders back and puffing out a deep breath into a little cloud ahead of me, I braced myself for impact and knocked.

Was I about to get a door slammed in my face? Would anyone even open the door in the first place? Or would he have a speech ready for me, one telling me to leave him alone and never speak to him again?

Would he cause a scene that stirred up the neighborhood? Would Eastwinders poke their heads out, braving the cold in their pajamas, to get a look at what all the fuss was about?

When he finally answered the door, my breath caught in my chest. He was dressed in navy blue cotton sweatpants and a gray long-sleeve shirt, and he stared down at me without an ounce of surprise.

"I owe you an explanation," I began, right as he said, "I'm sorry."

"Wait," I replied. "*You're* sorry? For what?"

"For yelling at you. I feel like a jerk. I scared you, I know. I can be... scary. I lost my temper, and I'm sorry. I never want to yell at you again."

"No, no, no," I said, shaking my head and trying to bring my mind back around to the speech I'd prepared on my walk over. "You don't need to be sorry."

"I absolutely do. I lose my temper sometimes, Dahlia, and there's no excuse. I hate that I lost it on you. I mean, to be fair, you lost it on me, but you're not scary. You're... well, you're small. I'm big. And I can turn into a bear."

"I'm pretty sure I can create zombies," I said.

His pained eyes went wide. "Wait, what?"

"Never mind. That's not why I'm here." I took a step closer to him and mustered all the gumption I could. I tried to imagine what my shade would do. She would probably slap him or something, and that would be too much, so I dialed it back a few notches, tried to extract the boldness without, you know, the physical violence. "I owe you an explanation of what happened in Stews and Brews. I made a wish without realizing it, and Liberty Freeman fulfilled it. I didn't mean for that to happen, but it did, and so even though it wasn't me who yelled at you, it sort of was."

Dante held up a hand. "What you just said... I don't understand any of that. Sounds like a long story, frankly. You'd better come inside."

"Oh. Right." I peeked past him into the dim living room where only a small lamp lit the space. "There's not, uh, anyone else in there. I'm not interrupting... anything?"

He glared at me. "If you think for one second that I have another woman over, the cold has clearly addled your brain. Get in here."

I refrained from saying, "yes, sir," and hurried past him into the warm space.

"You're alone, then?" I said.

"Yes, I'm alone," he snapped. "For fang's sake. Will you knock it off?" Then his tone softened, and he said, "I'm making tea. Want some?"

"I really need you to hear what I have to say," I protested.

"I'll hear it better with some caffeine in me. I'll make you a cup."

He disappeared into the kitchen, and without knowing fully what else to do, I hung up my coat and settled onto a corner of his sofa.

While I hadn't exactly been over to a bunch of bachelors' homes over the years, I'd heard stereotypes about them—they were sparse, dirty, devoid of anything on the walls except for posters lacking frames.

Dante's home was nothing like that. Every time I'd come over, it'd been clean. If I'd suspected that it was an act, that he only cleaned up when he was expecting a guest, I could let go of that belief now. I'd dropped in on him, yet his place was as clean and organized as ever.

A soft rug of rich browns, greens, and reds covered the center of the wood floor, and stretched out below the tan sofa and two hunter green armchairs. The fireplace across from me had logs stacked in it, ready for use, and on the mantle above was a collection of elegantly glazed geometric vases and lidded jars that he'd thrown himself at the studio. The way he'd set them out created a beautiful balance between the disparate sizes and shapes and reminded me of a city skyline at sunset.

His walls were covered not only in hanging pots with vines spilling over the edges, but framed photographs of his family and friends within the werebear clan. They smiled and laughed silently from the smoothly moving images, as the lamp light danced over their features. Would I ever be one of the people in those photographs?

"Okay," came his voice from behind me as he brought in two steaming cups from the kitchen. He placed one on the coffee table in front of me and the other on a small side table next to the hunter green chair he settled himself in. "I'll take that explanation now. The full one. Preferably long enough for it to make sense. Liberty Freeman has something to do with why you yelled at me?"

I closed my eyes to mentally reverse. My tendency to try to spew too many words at once had, yet again, caught up with me. It was like I either couldn't find the words I needed or found them all at once. I tried to think back to where this whole mess started.

"At the Blue Sky Festival," I began, "I was talking with Liberty Freeman after the feast. It was when you were talking with... other people."

"Izzy," he said.

"Right. Her. I was helping people clean up and... well, we were talking about standing up for ourselves and asking for what we wanted. I said something along the lines of 'I wish I knew how to say 'no' to people,' and Liberty took that literally."

"Yeah, he's a genie. Did you not know genies grant wishes?"

"Well, I did. I mean, it's probably the only thing I really knew about genies before coming to Eastwind. But I thought you had to rub the lamp they were trapped in or something, and then they were forced to grant you three wishes."

Dante cringed. "That sounds like slavery. Slavery isn't legal in Eastwind and hasn't been for a long time. Since Liberty got here, actually."

"Okay, well, I'm just telling you that I didn't know much about genies. I didn't realize he would take my wish so seriously."

"Don't you *want* people to take your wishes seriously?" he asked.

"Dante," I said, feeling a refreshing bit of frustration bubbling up, "I'm trying to explain what happened so you aren't mad at me about the restaurant."

"Right, right." He sipped his tea and leaned back.

"When you came and yelled at me at Time to Kiln, I truly didn't know what had happened. I was at the studio all night trying to track down who'd been leaving dead animals for me to find."

"Wait, doing what?" Then he caught himself, shook his head, and leaned back again. "We'll come back to that."

"Whoever came and yelled at you, it wasn't me, but... it was sort of me. It was someone who looked like me. It took me a while to figure it out, but I finally put it together and realized that Liberty Freeman was behind everything. I went and confronted him about it—"

"You confronted a genie?" He appeared both concerned and impressed.

"Yes but let me finish. When I talked to him, he told me that whatever came and yelled at you at the restaurant was a shade he'd conjured."

"A ghost?"

"I thought that, too. But no. It's a shade... of me. A part of me that is me but isn't me. Or more like,"—I chewed the bottom of my lip, struggling to find the words— "It's a part of me that I don't *want* to be a part of me. It's still there, though."

Dante's brow furrowed. "You wanted to yell at me?"

I winced, scrunching up my nose. "Yeah, I guess I did. But I wasn't going to!"

"But the shade did." He paused, staring down at the

surface of his tea. When he looked back up at me, he said, "Why did you *want* to call me out in public? Did you really think I was going behind your back with Izzy, like the shade accused me of doing?"

I balled my fists in my lap, wishing I could snap my fingers like Liberty Freeman and magically fast forward to the end of this conversation where everything was resolved. But I couldn't. There was only one way out of this: through. The more honesty I could muster, the quicker we might be done with this once and for all. Would Dante appreciate the honesty? That was impossible to know. But he deserved it all the same.

"It's embarrassing to admit, but yes, I suppose I did wonder about that. Otherwise, the shade wouldn't have done what she did."

He let out a deep sigh, his shoulders slumping. "To be totally transparent, she tried. Izzy. Last night, she came over here and told me... I won't go into details. But she wanted to know if I was interested."

I couldn't breathe. I needed to know what happened next. Had he let her inside? Had he considered it?

"I'm not interested in her," he said. "I never was. I always thought she and I were just friends." I could feel the disappointment pulsing from him as he shook his head. "I'm an idiot, I guess. Since we were friends growing up, I figured that's all she would ever want to be. It's all I ever wanted to be. But she had other ideas. I'm sorry, Dahlia. You were right about suspecting something, but it wasn't coming from me. Looking at it now, yeah, we weren't acting like friends. She kept suggesting we hang out, and I kept agreeing. It never even crossed my mind to take things further with her because I didn't want to. She's a beautiful woman, but I'm not attracted to her in that way." I wanted to take him at face value, but there was guilt lingering around his words that I still couldn't place.

"What is it?" I asked. "You feel guilty, but you said you didn't know her intentions."

"She's a friend. Or was a friend. I led her on without knowing I was, and I hate that. She was just so embarrassed when I didn't reciprocate... Makes me feel like a bad person, even if I didn't mean to hurt anybody. Not her, not you. She's gone now. Headed back to Avalon. I hope she can forget this whole thing ever happened and find someone who's right for her. It's not me, though." He paused, and I let the silence simmer as I tried to process everything he was saying. "I know you said you're fine with keeping things casual, and I'm not going to push you, but you're the only person I want to be with, Dahlia. Not Izzy, not anyone else. If you want to keep your options open, I won't pressure you. Yeah, it'll hurt my feelings to see you spending time with other guys, but, well, I guess I deserve it after the last few days, and my feelings are my problem, not yours. If you want to keep things as they are, not rush into anything serious, I can respect that."

"I don't," I blurted. "I don't want that. I want...," I shut my eyes tight, begging myself to find the words, to understand what I really wanted. "I want you to be my boyfriend. I don't want us to date other people."

When I opened my eyes again, Dante was staring at me, a small grin on his tired face. "You sure?"

"Yes. Absolutely. That's what I want. You're who I want."

He set his tea to the side and sat next to me on the couch. "You're all I want, too." He tucked a thick curl behind my ear, his palm pressing against my cheek. "And if you ever need to yell at me again to remind me of that, you go right ahead."

His breath was warm on my cold nose as he leaned in. I closed my eyes and thanked the part of me that got us here, albeit in a chaotic fashion. As his soft lips met mine, I thanked my shade for going too far so that I could finally find this place, this *just right* place.

When he finally broke the kiss, the first thing out of his mouth was, "Now, what was that you said about being able to make zombies?"

CHAPTER NINETEEN

Atlas stayed close by my side as I hid behind the shelves of drying greenware in the studio and waited.

I'd spent most of the previous day sleeping, catching up after the all-night investigation. I owed Sasha one for covering my morning shift on such short notice.

While my sleep schedule was undeniably thrown off, it worked to my advantage in that it meant I could stake out the studio overnight without falling asleep like I had before.

I was also smart enough not to drink an entire bottle of wine this time. I was learning all kinds of lessons the hard way lately.

Atlas wasn't on the same sleep schedule that I was, and his head had slowly been drooping then shooting up again for the last two hours of the stakeout.

I'd followed Liberty Freeman's instructions, which seemed like a smart thing to do, and set out the open can of tuna on the floor as I lay in wait.

The pieces had come together for me to form a hypothesis that said I wasn't up against a powerful being, or even one close to my size, and that I wasn't in any real danger. I still had yet to test that hypothesis, though.

Not long after the short hand of the clock inched past the four, I spotted movement while I peered between two large bowls on the shelf.

It all made sense now how someone could've come and gone without waking up Atlas or me on our first attempt at catching whoever was leaving me dead animals. The answer to that mystery was simple: the culprit was silent on its feet.

Or rather, its *paws*.

The gray tabby cat slunk into view, inching toward the open can of tuna. While Liberty's suggestion of leaving tuna had tipped me off to the fact that I might be dealing with a feline intruder, what I hadn't expected was to recognize him.

I nudged Atlas awake, holding a finger to my lips as I nodded toward where the cat was inching toward the can.

It had something in its mouth, and as soon as it was close enough to get a strong sniff of the tuna, it dropped what was in its jaws. A small mouse hit the floor and wasted no time in scurrying away, apparently no worse for the wear and very much alive.

Atlas's hackles shot up as he, too, spotted the tabby. I motioned for him to stay put, and then I tiptoed as quietly as I could around the shelves to nab the cat without scaring him off.

I was close, nearly within arm's reach, when he must've sensed me. He dropped low to the floor, whipping his head around before jumping nearly three feet in the air.

"It's okay!" I assured him. "Givens, it's okay! I'm not going to hurt you!"

"My witch promised the same things, and she hurt me very badly!"

"I know she did," I said, holding out my hands to let him know I wasn't trying anything. "She tried to hurt me too, remember?"

It was something I could never forget. His witch, Gloriana, had been the innkeeper at what was formerly Muscoff Manor Inn, now Malavic Manor Inn. I'd been asked to investigate a murder there alongside Nora only a few months earlier, and while I'd solved it, it wasn't without facing down a very dangerous witch—Givens' witch. But Gloriana was now living out the foreseeable future in Iron-helm Penitentiary for having conjured a spirit that caused an innocent elf's death and then attempting to kill me as well.

I hadn't considered what might happen to a familiar if their witch was locked away, but now I couldn't avoid asking the question. "How are you free?"

"She severed ties with me," he replied, bowing his head. *"She cut our connection. I'm no longer her familiar. I'm just... a spare part."*

My heart broke for him. "She must not have wanted to see you spend your life in Ironhelm," I said, trying to offer some small comfort.

"It wasn't that. She said I disgusted her. All I did was get underfoot. She blames me for letting you get away."

I crouched down to be more on his level. "I'm so sorry."

"It's for the best. She was awful to me. You can't imagine what it was like being connected with someone like her. Black heart, that one. She poured it into me."

I wanted nothing more than to scoop up his little scrawny body into my arms and hold and comfort him, but I knew he wouldn't allow that. Too much love and comfort after none at all would likely feel intolerable to him. Instead, I asked, "Why have you been leaving dead animals for me? Are you angry with me for getting your witch arrested? I would understand if you were."

"Angry? No! I'm thankful. I don't bring gifts to just anyone. I wanted to show my appreciation."

"That's very sweet of you," I replied, trying not to cry at the full sweetness of his gifts. Never mind that I didn't want any dead animals. In this case, it truly was the thought that counted. "But why have you been hiding?"

His eyes darted toward where Atlas was still crouched behind a shelf. *"Your dog is very big."*

"I'm not a dog," Atlas replied from his hiding place. *"I'm a hellhound. And a big scary one at that. You really don't want to mess with me."*

I leaned toward Givens, and whispered, "I'll let you in on a little secret. He's as scared of you as you are of him."

"Not true," Atlas replied. *"I'm very big and brave. Best not to, uh, come mess with me. And don't even try to bop me on the head!"*

I shrugged at Givens who appeared to relax.

"That tuna is for you," I said.

"No thanks," the tabby replied. *"It's clearly a trap."*

"It was never a trap," I said, "more of a lure. But it's perfectly good to eat. See, I'll try some." I pinched off a bit, and while I'd never been a huge fan of tuna, eating it was for a good cause. I put it in my mouth and chewed. "Mmm... See? Totally okay. And now that I know who you are, I'd love for you to eat it. Don't take this the wrong way, but you're skin and bones."

"That's because I'm not used to catching my own food."

"But you caught all those mice. And that snake and bird."

"I don't know how to prepare them, though. What, am I supposed to eat them with the fur and bones in?"

I couldn't help but smile. My initial assessment when I met Givens back at the inn was that he was a mean old thing. But now I had a better measure of him, and it was clear he was, after all, just a cat who adapted to the witch he lived with. And that witch happened to be a poisonous murderess. Not his fault. If he could learn to be sour, he could learn to be kind. And even if he stayed sour for the rest of his days, he still deserved to have adequate food and shelter.

"That's a good point," I replied. "I wouldn't want to eat anything with the fur and bones. But this tuna doesn't have that." I paused. "You know, the studio has a lot of mice that run around and get into the materials. I was just talking to one of the owners, Raven, about it. We could really use someone who could chase off those mice. If you're interested, I could talk to her and see if she'd like to bring you on as a studio cat, maybe provide a little security in return for all the food and water you need?"

"You saved me from Gloriana. If you want me to kill a thousand mice, I'm obliged to do so."

"No, no, no," I said. "You don't need to *kill* any mice. Just chase them away. And only during the nights, when the place is empty. When people are around, the mice will stay away. I can get you a nice, soft cat bed to sleep on inside during the day. And if you wake up and want some pets, you can come out and say hello to the students during the classes. Just, you know, maybe don't shed on their clay projects."

"What if I don't chase any mice away the night before? Will I still be fed?"

"What? Yes! Of course. You'll be fed every day, regardless of the work you did the night before."

Givens hissed. *"That doesn't sound right. What's in it for you?"*

I blinked. "Nothing."

"Doesn't sound right at all. There has to be something in it for you."

I chewed on the inside of my lip, thinking. He had a point, and if I were going to pretend otherwise, I might end up with another shade walking around, pretending to be me. "I guess knowing you're taken care of and have a home helps me believe that the world is a kind and gentle place where people take care of each other. And that helps me believe that people might take care of me instead of casting me aside if I ever really needed it. Helping you makes me feel a little less scared of being all alone again, like I used to be."

"You used to be all alone? You didn't always have your hellhound?"

I shook my head. "I'm new to Eastwind. I used to live somewhere else where no one ever noticed me and I crept around out of sight. It was how I stayed safe. I guess. But now I'm here, and people see me; and while it's sometimes scary, it's worth feeling less alone." I scooted the tuna can toward him, and after a moment's pause, he padded to it, leaned down his bony little head, and took his first bite. After that, I was pretty sure he couldn't have stopped himself from finishing off the whole thing if he tried.

"*I guess we'll find out if it was poisoned soon enough,*" he said, licking the inside of the now-empty can.

"I guess so. And when you realize it wasn't, will you trust that I mean you no harm?"

"We'll see," he said. "*But I bet I'll trust you a little more once I try out that cat bed you mentioned.*"

"And Raven agreed to the setup?" Dante asked as I finished laying out the hot sandwiches I'd brought over to his apartment from Hagseed Café for lunch the following day.

"Without hesitation," I replied. "I asked her as soon as she walked in this morning, and she said 'absolutely'." I leaned forward, even though it was only the two of us eating around his coffee table. "Apparently, she and Gloriana were in the same class at Mancer Academy back in the day and never liked one another. Giving shelter to Gloriana's familiar and treating him better than Gloriana ever did is the kind of revenge Raven prefers."

Dante laughed. "Can't argue with that. And if it also solves her problem and Givens' problem at the same time, even better."

"Don't forget about my problem," I added. "I kept finding dead animals."

"Oh right. The zombies." He grimaced. "Glad you don't have to deal with that anymore."

"That makes two of us. Oh, and I checked in with Zoe Clementine. The bird I brought to her is already healed and back out in the wild. She really has a gift for helping animals."

As he lifted one half of his sandwich to his mouth, I said, "Hold on there. I have one more thing for us." I reached in my bag, pulled out the teapot he made me and two mugs I'd borrowed from the studio. "Ruby taught me how to make a proper cup of tea."

He grinned. "Oh yeah? Need me to grab some loose leaf?"

"Actually," I said, "no. I brought my own."

"Ah! Even mixing your own now!"

"Not really," I said, playing innocent. "Ruby gave me one of hers. I think she stole the recipe from A New Leaf. Apropos of nothing, you don't have to work this afternoon, right?"

He narrowed his eyes at me with deep suspicion. "No, why?"

"And do you like to dance?"

Now he looked plain confused. "Why are you asking me all these questions?"

"Oh, no reason. I'll get a kettle started. You go ahead and start on your sandwich. I've been told this tea is best enjoyed on a bit of a full stomach."

It clicked for him, and he guffawed. "Dahlia! I had no idea you were so adventurous!"

I glanced back at him on my way to the kitchen. "If there's one thing you should know about me, Dante, it's that I'm a girl who knows what she wants." ☾

Murder's on tap at the pub. Can Dahlia's new powers brew up answers? Read SOUL GLAZE, the fourth book of the Dahlia Wildes Magical Mysteries.

A NOTE FROM NOVA

Thank you for joining Dahlia and me for this one. It's certainly one of the lighter books I've written, purposefully omitting a murder. I don't mind murder, generally (please don't take that out of context), but this was the first book I wrote following the death of my beloved dog Penny, who stayed by my side through dark winters that threatened never to pass.

I said goodbye to her the day after *Deadly Inn-Tensions* released, and I wrote this book under thick gray clouds, desperate for a Blue Sky Festival of my own to roll around. When it finally did, it arrived in the most unexpected way. My grief from losing Penny seemed to have exacerbated some ongoing health problems I've been living with for the last fifteen years. I'd been struggling to get any doctors to take the symptoms seriously, and if I'm completely honest, I'd started telling myself it was nothing, too. It was "normal" to feel this bad, right? But I couldn't pretend anymore once the grief set in and threw my health into chaos. I found a new doctor and she took me seriously. Not only do

I finally have a diagnosis, but I'm on treatment that has changed my life. I've seen the blue sky overhead again. I couldn't have gotten there if it weren't for Penny and the bond we shared for fifteen years that led to such intense grief.

Eastwinders like us know that it's never "just a dog" or "just a cat." These are our familiars. In Eastwind, they live as long as their witches. I wish it were the same on Earth. That said, Penny's made it clear that she's still around in other ways, and always will be. I'm grateful to her for sticking around.

I'm also grateful to you for sticking around. There are a lot of tales from Eastwind, and you keep coming back to visit. Your support has remained a constant in my life, and I appreciate that so much.

I'll be back in the next book with some serious crime, I'm sure, but in the meantime, I hope you've enjoyed this lighter read. If you're one of the many who've been living with thick clouds overhead, I hope you enjoy a blue sky soon.

-Nova

THANK YOU!

I'm so grateful that you took a chance on Dahlia! If you loved the book, the kindest thing you can do is take a moment to leave an Amazon review so others might also give it a chance.

Even a simple, "Will definitely keep reading this series!" goes a long way.

Leave your review here:
https://readerlinks.com/l/4330267

Thanks so much, and I hope you enjoy the next book!
-Nova

JOIN THE COZY COVEN

GET 1 NOVELLA AND 4 SHORT STORIES FROM
EASTWIND WHEN YOU SIGN UP

GO TO THECOZYCOVEN.COM

Head here to join the festivities:
https://www.eastwindwitches.com/cozy-coven

ABOUT THE AUTHOR

Nova Nelson grew up on a steady diet of Agatha Christie novels. She loves the mind candy of cozy mysteries and has been weaving paranormal tales since she first learned handwriting. Those two loves meet in her Eastwind Witches series, and it's about time, if she does say so herself.

When she's not busy writing, she enjoys long walks with her strong-willed dogs and eating breakfast for dinner.

Say hello:
nova@novanelson.com

facebook.com/thecozycoven

instagram.com/authornovanelson

bookbub.com/authors/nova-nelson

goodreads.com/nova_nelson

amazon.com/author/novanelson

The Eastwind Witches Cozy Mysteries

Crossing Over Easy (Book 1)

Death Metal (Book 2)

Third Knock the Charm (Book 3)

Queso de los Muertos (Book 4)

Psych-Out (Book 5)

Gone Witch (Book 6)

Love Spells Trouble (Book 7)

Storm A-Brewin' (Book 8)

Hallow's Faire in Love and War (Book 9)

Dead Witch Walking (Book 10)

Old Haunts (Book 11)

First-Realm Problems (Book 12)

Happily Hereafter (Book 13)

The Ruby True Magical Mysteries

Werebear Scare (Book 1)

Elves' Bells (Book 2)

Vampire's Ire (Book 3)

The Dahlia Wildes Magical Mysteries

Time to Kiln (Book 1)

Deadly Inn-Tensions (Book 2)

Throwing Shades (Book 3)

Find them here: www.eastwindwitches.com

www.ingramcontent.com/pod-product-compliance
Lightning Source LLC
Chambersburg PA
CBHW030142010826
48973CB00002B/687